T0067983

White GODS Black DEMONS

White GODS

BLACK Demons

by

DANIEL MANDISHONA

WEAVER
PRESS

First published by
Weaver Press, Box A1922, Avondale, Harare, 2009
<www.weaverpresszimbabwe.com>

This revised edition, 2018

© Daniel Mandishona, 2009, 2018

Typeset by Weaver Press
Cover Design: Harare.
Printed by: Bidvest, South Africa.
Distributed in South Africa by Jacana Media

All rights reserved. No part of the publication may be
reproduced, stored in a retrieval system or transmitted
in any form by any means – electronic, mechanical,
photocopying, recording, or otherwise – without
the express written permission of the publisher.

ISBN: 978-1-77922-333-3 (p/b)
ISBN: 978-1-77922-334-0 (e-pub)

Daniel Mandishona is an architect. He was born in Harare in 1959 and brought up by his maternal grandparents in Mbare township (then known as Harari township). In 1976 he was expelled from Goromonzi Secondary School and lived in London from 1977-1992. He first studied Graphic Design then Architecture at the Bartlett School, University College London. He now has his own practice in Harare. His first short story, 'A Wasted Land' was published in *Contemporary African Short Stories* (Heineman,1992)

They stole our sleep in a daylight siege
And in our brief madness we
Exchanged lullabies for anguished cries.

'Ghosts' – Kofi Anyidoho

Contents

1

Smoke and Ashes

You won the elections, but I won the count.

(Anastasio Somoza, former Nicaraguan President, after a
losing opponent had accused him of having rigged a poll.)

Dreams are wiser than men, my daughter...

Venus, the history of our country is written in blood.

Your father is one of our country's heroes. I remember him
well, a small magisterial man with a sweet tongue and a weakness
for colourful ties. Smart and elegant, he loved to dress like the
American gangsters of the Prohibition era. Those baggy suits, so
voluminous he looked like an inflatable doll. The ubiquitous Van
Dyke beard, always trimmed to perfection; and that big oblong
head, the rumoured depository of a formidable intellect – a couple
of excellent first degrees, Master's degree in Politics, MBA, Ph.D.
in Mathematics. Samson Erasmus Mate; he was the local boy who
made good. He was a true hero of the masses. But Venus, true
heroism is not like a bolt of lightning or a freak snowfall, something
that comes and goes with the weather.

In his day they used violence as a tool to unseat the renegade
regime. They threw Molotov cocktails and torched cars. They
vandalised communications and smeared belligerent graffiti on

1

the walls of public buildings. *Majority Rule. One man one vote.* The educated ones, those who called themselves 'nationalists', directed the anger of the masses, pinpointing the regime's most vulnerable targets with unerring accuracy. Sometimes anarchy and guile can work in tandem. Then the war came to the cities. The enemy had too many places in which to hide. The soldiers patrolled the township like an angry army of occupation. There was a dusk-to-dawn curfew, a shoot-to-kill policy. Questions can be asked later, because the dead cannot argue.

Later in his life, long after retirement, your father became active in politics again. Things were in a bad way, he said. The country needed him, the small man who always rose to the big occasions. But this time it would be against his own people, against his own kind and against his own conscience. Perhaps by accident, or by design, your father had metamorphosed into a political chameleon, forever floating on the winds of opportunity. He always believed that politics was the one route that offered him the final opportunity to distinguish himself. Hope springs eternal, Venus, everything has its own time.

But his time had long passed. He was a relic of a forgotten era, the lone dinosaur that survived the mass extinctions.

When the election date was announced he declared himself an independent candidate and took to the campaign trail with a zeal that surprised all of us. For so long the reluctant revolutionary, he couldn't afford to wait any longer. In politics, procrastination is often the child of indecision. Patience is not always a virtue. He said his time had finally come. In the fifties he had been a thorn in the side of the regime, a firebrand agitator who feared nothing. But there were others whose oratory skills surpassed his. There were others more intellectually gifted than he was. Barely thirty, he contested for the leadership of the party and lost. Dejected, he disappeared from the political scene, retreated into the oblivion of a monastic existence. But this time round he said he represented a new dawn. He boasted that he was the one beacon of hope amidst the mounting confusion.

I alone have a plan to rescue my people from this morass, he said. I alone have the road map to the Promised Land.

But it was a fatal error. We all knew that was the end of whatever political dreams he might still have harboured. A man once capable of leading his nation to greatness, he had endured four years of solitary detention in a bush prison and come out a broken man. He might have worn the scars of the wounds inflicted by his tormentors like badges of honour and bragged about his spirit's resilience, but we all knew his frail ambitions had long withered in the first fires of self-doubt that beset him during that unbearable incarceration. Now, buttressed by empty rhetoric and an indefatigable self-belief, he boldly entered the fray, made the usual promises and gave the usual pledges.

But there was scepticism; there was doubt. After all this was a man who, politically, had long been discredited, diminished and defeated. Not surprisingly, very few people took him seriously. Those who knew him from the early days wrote scathing letters to the press – beware the kiss of Judas, for this was a man who once ran with the hares and hunted with the hounds. He was a pariah, an ogre; he couldn't be trusted. And yet, how quickly the effervescent laudations of yesteryear had become the shrill denouncements of the present! The younger voters were also intrigued. Who is this man? Where did he come from? What does he stand for?

Tell us, what will you do about unemployment? What will you do about poverty? What about hunger? What about AIDS? Will there be enough schools for our children? Will there be enough hospitals for the sick?

We will cross that bridge when we come to it, he said. But some bridges are unreachable, Venus. Some bridges are un-crossable. We knew he would lose and then regret his rash actions. Independents in our country are an unknown species; the political turf is well defined, the battlefields clearly demarcated. There is no middle ground.

Ultimately, all elections are about winning. As somebody once said, winning isn't everything – it's the only thing. Everybody remembers who came first, nobody remembers who came second. And our throwaway Bluetooth culture has a way of permanently archiving also-rans to the dustbin of history. Failure will always be the prerogative of mediocrity.

A long time ago we lived in the same township.

Our parents were friends. Your mother said you were named after the Italian goddess of love and fertility. Or was it the goddess of gardens and spring? You were pretty and popular, the star of our limited universe. We turned a popular hit tune into a praise-song about you and a legendary soccer player whose silky skills had been honed in the township dirt. And most days after school we ran home in single file, shouting out our own bastardised chorus of that song:

I am your Venus... I am your fire... George Shaya...

George Shaya, the 'Mastermind'. The lynchpin of a team supported by millions. The football commentators used to drool over his dribbling skills, equating him to a hot knife slicing through butter. Nimble-footed and mercurial, opposing defenders couldn't get anywhere near him. He was as elusive as Osama bin Laden.

One day your father took us to the Kopje and showed us the place where in 1890 the British planted their flag in the African soil in the name of a distant monarch. He told us about the woman who led the uprising against the colonists in 1896, Nehanda. She was a spirit medium, but the British, who had no knowledge of our Shona culture, called her a witch. They hanged her for treason, and those who witnessed the event said she went to the gallows with commendable fortitude.

You and I went to the same primary and secondary schools. You and I had the same friends when we were infants, when we were teenagers, and when we became adults. You and I did the same B.Comm. degree at the University of Zimbabwe, starting together and finishing together in the same year. You graduated with distinction. I had to make do with a lower second. After varsity you and I worked for the same bank. In our free time you and I did the same things in the same places with the same people.

When your uncle Philemon 'Killer' Mate took up boxing we used to go and watch his early fights together. He was a useful light middleweight, with a deadly left hook and a chin like a rock. Nobody ever knocked him off his feet up to the day he retired. But like your father, he was not destined for greatness. Although he made a decent living from the fury of his fists, we all knew he would never shake the world. After he retired from boxing uncle 'Killer' used his savings to start a panel-beating business that also repaired cracked windscreens. Mangled cars were not a problem, as most people in the townships had no licences, drank and drove and were always getting involved in accidents. Cracked windscreens were a different matter altogether.

In the early days, business was so erratic uncle 'Killer' used to hire the township's petty miscreants, arm them with catapults, and then dispatch them on clandestine missions to go around cracking the windscreens of parked cars. The vandals thoughtfully left uncle's business cards stuck under the windscreen wipers. A location map was generously provided on the reverse side of the cards. Another of his employment creation schemes involved deliberately plying tarred roads with grit to increase the incidence of cracked windscreens. Unfortunately, one of the early casualties of these underhand activities was uncle 'Killer' himself, when a loose stone on the streets cracked the windscreen of his treasured blue and gold 1967 VW Beetle.

We were never lovers, but when we were in primary school you sometimes let me put my head between your legs and smell your privates. You said the game was called 'fellatio', and you had seen it in a pornographic Swedish magazine uncle 'Killer' kept under his bed. We stopped this silly game after a knotted sheaf of your pubic hairs strayed into my eye. The pain was like having a fresh boil lanced with a toothpick. It was difficult to explain to my mother what I had been doing when the injury happened. We were together in the high school play, an exhausting Shakespearean tragedy we performed on Parents' Day. I remember you had one of the best lines:

Fair is foul, and foul is fair. Hover through the fog and filthy air.

But like those dark tragedies of the Bard of Avon, our lives will always be a symphony of discords. Ours is an imperfect world because we always view it through the cracked mirrors around us. Something magical was supposed to happen between us but it never did. But there is still time. Life is not an exact science. Nothing is cast in stone, Venus, nothing is ever what it seems to be.

When you were in your mid-twenties there was an economic downturn in the country; you said things were not working for you. In 1998, you were one of a lucky few; you won a green card in the lottery run by the American embassy. You could live in America, the land of your dreams, without the necessary immigration papers. You could become a legal alien.

But none of us were surprised by your good fortune because even when you were a toddler, we all knew your moment of greatness was coming. We all knew there were wonderful things in store for you. When you resigned from the bank we threw you an unforgettable farewell party at a city centre hotel the day you left. You left the country that same year to start a new and exciting life in a strange land. Now you live in some remote backwater in the deepest part of the Deep South.

In 2002, you quietly married a Harvard educated professor of nutrition, a fellow countryman. But I don't think it's a happy marriage. He was not exactly the Prince Charming of your wet dreams. You don't talk much about him, except that in 2004 he wrote a best-selling book on dieting – *Why Fat Doesn't Stick To The Roof Of Your Mouth And Other Culinary Secrets*. One by one, all your siblings have followed you to America, visiting on holidays and never coming back.

Identification papers, social security numbers, work permits, welfare cards – you know how to manipulate the system. You know how to create ghosts out of the living. Your eldest sister Penelope is the only one who never joined you in America. She married a schoolteacher twice her age and became a counsellor of teenage mothers. She now has a flighty teenage daughter of her own to contend with.

Friday, 21st March 2008

You recently sent me an e-mail – you wanted me to pick you up from the airport on Sunday afternoon. You were coming back home for one purpose, and for one specific purpose only: *I want to vote. I want my voice to count. I want change.* But it's been ten years. You are not sure whether your name is still on the voters' roll. The only way to find out is on the day itself. But your mother said things are now so bad here, it's a risk you are willing to take.

Picked you up from the airport on a cold Sunday afternoon. In the car, cutting across the deserted city centre, we discussed life's ups and downs, existence's transient discomforts. How we two so far have endured this mortal coil. You talked very little and listened a lot. You nodded your head, compliant like a ventriloquist's dummy. You remarked on the quaintness of the city's crumbling colonial buildings, as if you were seeing them for the first time. Perhaps your exposure to foreign climes had sharpened your perception of your surroundings, finally lifted the dense Third World fog from your vision.

You remarked on the devil-may-care attitude of the city's inhabitants, the rude unwashed urchins begging for money at crowded intersections. And the currency, the Mickey Mouse currency! The more zeroes it acquires, the less it buys, you said. Yes, I agreed. I remember the time, barely a year ago, when a million dollars used to be called a 'metre' in the amorphous slang of the townships, because that was the distance one million dollars' worth of groceries covered when spread on the ground. Now a million dollars cannot buy anything, because even a single cigarette costs five billion dollars.

Your largest note is fifty billion dollars, you scoffed, and it cannot buy a decent lunch. It cannot even buy a soda.

Yes, I humbly agreed, this is a country of poor millionaires and destitute billionaires. I noticed your use of the second person singular, the subtle distancing of your newly Americanised soul from a country in the throes of a desperate economic meltdown. Now that you are the holder of a green card and you live on a bayou on the edge of the Mississippi, it would seem you are no longer one of us. And it's no longer soft drinks and biscuits at the Italian Bakery for you, but sodas and cookies.

To cheer me up, you made an attempt at humour: do you know that a survey conducted in America said Sweden was the happiest nation and ours was the saddest? Do you know that people in Moldova, Guatemala, Albania, Turkmenistan and Somalia are happier than us? It's not funny, but I laugh because you expect me to. The preceding week that joke had been text-messaged to me by about forty people. But you didn't know that. At the traffic lights a young vagrant thrusts a dirty hand through the half-open window. You visibly recoil at the stench from his armpits.

Asking for help, madam. Please, can you give me only ten billion dollars?

You stare open-mouthed at the boy, your mind boggled by the astronomical figure you have just heard. I pass you a crisp five hundred-million-dollar note. You offer it to the young boy. He shrugs his bare shoulders, a gesture of rejection.

Don't give me sick money madam, he says. Five hundred million doesn't buy me anything. Okay, if ten is too much just give me five billion.

I have no more money. Go away.

The little creature snarls, baring a mouthful of uneven yellow teeth. His parting shot is a shocking expletive – *mhata ya amai vako* – your mother's so-and-so.

The lights turn to green. I cannot drive off fast enough.

The vocalist from Led Zeppelin is wailing on the car radio.

I have been dazed and confused…
So have you.

We drive towards your city centre hotel. We pass the old cinema on Nkrumah Avenue that is now used by a Pentecostal church known for its rabid followers and all-night prayer meetings. Many years ago, we once watched an old James Bond movie at the cinema. You laughed throughout because one of the characters was called Pussy Galore. The hotel used to be a five-star establishment but now the only stars in it are the fake ones painted on the ceiling of the buffet restaurant. There is a karaoke bar next door, always packed, always rowdy. A discordant wail painfully hurtles itself through the open windows.

… And ah-aaaaaaaaaaaaaaah will always love yoooooooooooo-oooo … Huuuuu-uuuuu …

You laugh and shake your luxuriantly artificial dreadlocks. But I can see you have changed. You are not the Venus of 1998. In 2008, you have become more streetwise, more sophisticated – a spruced-up vintage model. The crooked bridge of the nose is now straight, your lips narrower, meaner – plastic surgery, perhaps? In America, where there is everything – your words, not mine, Venus – anything is possible.

But I want to close my eyes; to see you as the picture of innocence I remember from our youth. I want to imagine, to fantasise, to dream, of the old you. But somehow, I know it will never be. You are a different you; you are a new you I don't really know. You are not the Venus from our crèche days who knew all the stories by Hans Christian Andersen and the Brothers Grimm and Enid Blyton. The loudmouthed girl eager to impress the teachers by memorising all the nursery rhymes:

Rapunzel, Rapunzel… Let down your hair, so I can climb without a stair…

No, you belong to a past we slowly detached ourselves from a long time ago, like dew rising from the grass. Whatever was meant to happen between us is irretrievably gone. It's now all smoke and ashes. What was that you always said about the nature of existence, the purpose of life?

If there is no past there can be no future.

Or some such words to that effect.

26ᵗʰ March 2008

Three days before the Election.

The President is on the television news, rallying the masses somewhere deep in the bedrock of the Revolution. Down with the British, down with the Americans. Bush and Brown, those terrible Imperialist twins, must leave us alone. Our history is written in blood; we will never sell our birthright. This is the Final Battle of Control. This is hundred per cent Total War. The path to true Independence is strewn with obstacles.

But we will never be a colony again.

A luta continua.

27ᵗʰ March 2008

You asked me to take you to the main bus terminus because you wanted to visit your grandfather who lives in the rural areas. You have not seen him for ten years. The buses crowding the concourse are crammed with passengers and it is hard to determine at first glance which buses are leaving, which ones are arriving and which ones are just stationary. Touts employed by the bus owners vie for customers, pushing and jostling and sometimes even exchanging blows.

The fights are short and decisive, and before one realises what has happened things go back to where they were a few moments earlier. The bus you are boarding has barely ground to a halt before a motley army of vendors invade it, with even more waiting outside. They rush to every new arrival the way ants swarm a fallen fig. This is what poverty has done to our once proud nation.

Outside the bus you have to bravely endure the persuasive overtures of more grim-faced vendors noisily advertising wares nobody wants to buy – from bottled love potions to dubious Malawian aphrodisiacs, from get-rich-quick charms to metal bracelets that will enable the wearer to accurately forecast the correct numbers of the next trillion-dollar Lotto. Some of the more determined vendors are callously stepping over the unmarketable oddments of their comrades lining the dusty tarmac, initiating furious arguments that are frequently accompanied by curses, pushes and shoves.

I will be back after two days, you shout amidst the chaos.

28th March 2008

I am in my two-bedroom flat on the King George Road. No water, no electricity. No power for two full days now; water has been gone for twenty-six hours. When it comes back it will be an unsightly trickle barely able to fill a pot. There is an unwritten rule that the toilet is flushed once a day, late in the evening when everybody's ablution requirements have been completed. We all live in fear of a cholera outbreak. Last night we couldn't cook and had to make do with Chinese takeaways for the second night in a row. There is no official explanation for the blackout. Nobody says anything about the water.

The maid, Maria, went on leave. She was supposed to have gone for four days. She has been gone for six. I cannot wait for the story; she always comes back with a sob story, Maria. Always funerals to attend, always sick relatives to visit. But she has a poor memory, and more often than not becomes a victim of her own fabrications. So far, her father has died twice in four years and an aunt has had cerebral malaria three times. Last year a sister who had perished in a train disaster turned up on my doorstep. Robin, my seven-year-old son, is struggling with his Grade 2 arithmetic. Most of the times he has to do his homework by candlelight. The sums don't make much sense. *Tom had ten dollars. He gave Jane nine dollars. How much did he have left?*

Daddy, was there a time when one dollar used to buy something? he always asks.

I drive Robin and a neighbour's son to school and the neighbour brings them back at lunchtime. His mother takes him for the weekends and half the holidays. It's an arrangement that works like clockwork. Our marriage foundered after four stormy years. It was an unhappy time for all of us and the less said, the better.

All the vendors along the road to Robin's school seem to be selling toilet paper. Which is strange, really, comments Robin, since there isn't that much food around. I agree. Toilet paper implies full stomachs that at some stage will need to be emptied. But when you are hungry the last thing you want to see is toilet paper. After dropping Robin off, I have to go and wait for you at the main bus terminus. You are coming back today.

Tomorrow is the big one. Tomorrow is D-Day.

That evening, at your invitation, I came to visit you at the hotel. We drank a lot of alcohol and you told me about the Cajun delights of your Louisiana town, Ponchatoula. It's not even really a town, you said. More like a village with modern conveniences. We watched a championship fight between a black boxer and a white boxer on one of the sports channels. The black boxer won by a knockout in the second round.

The predominantly white audience threw plastic cups and beer cans into the ring. Then we watched an old horror on the movie channel, a story about aliens set in outer space. Both of us have always loved the adrenalin rush that comes with well-crafted cinematic suspense. *In Space no one can hear you scream,* said the blurb on the publicity posters when the film first came out in the early eighties.

Afterwards we went to a nightclub, Room Ten. Or was it Room Twelve? You know me – I have never been very good with figures. They play excellent rhythm and blues, you insisted. Not really my cup of tea, though. I'm strictly into roots reggae, rock steady and dancehall – the Gladiators, Israel Vibration, Steel Pulse. *Natty dread never run away... Dis ya ah prophecy...*

Despite my feeble protestations that age has finally caught up with me, you drag me onto the dance floor and force me to dance. I perform a half-remembered semi-erotic jig from our secondary school days. We used to call it 'the zombie shuffle', a surreal routine that involved rigorously swaying the pelvis whilst the feet remained resolutely rooted to the same spot. As if to add insult to considerable injury, you insist on shouting the song's monosyllabic chorus into my ear throughout.

Under my umbrella… rella rella ella ella ella ella ella eh eh eh eh eh eh eh…

I drive you back to your hotel in the small hours. Your tired head lolls on my shoulder, your plaited hair soft and jasmine scented. For some reason, I think of the naughty game we used to play in the moonlit township streets – 'fellatio'. Above us the full moon, crisp and bone-white, streaks silently through the pristine cradle of the heavens. Ahead of us a long-distance lorry grinds uphill like a tired animal. I am playing *Shaking on the Bayou*, the excellent Champion Jack Dupree CD you bought for me at JFK Airport on your way in. After our frenetic activities on the crowded Room Ten dance floor, nothing could be more soothing to our tortured muscles.

At the hotel we talk about the forthcoming election, the rapidly nose-diving economy and our friends dispersed in the Diaspora.

Forget politics, and do something meaningful with your life, you said – a clearly calculated provocation.

I am a staunch member of the party. I am not into all this regime-change rubbish. We want progress, but not change.

Honestly, I have never understood how people like you function.

Let's just say man is a creature of mystery. That he cannot begin to understand the world around him until he understands himself. Ha! Ha! Ha!

You are drunk. But honestly, you need to reform that fossilised institution of yours if you are going to win this election.

We will win this election hands down. Mark my words.

Seriously, you should think about coming to America. I can always arrange papers.

Thanks, but I like it here.

There you go again. If you stay here, your life will be over before you know it.

Maybe, but I can't go anywhere. We are fighting a new war.

What war?

We are fighting neo-imperialism and its black puppets. The British cannot tell us what to do. We are a sovereign state.

That maybe so, but sovereignty means nothing without democracy.

Are you saying this country is not democratic?

I'm saying the democratic space is very limited. We fought for one man, one vote – not for every man to vote for one man.

Meaning?

We are denied our freedoms. Freedom of speech is a right, not a privilege. Do you know that in America there is something called the First Amendment? The law actually protects you to say what you want to say, however unpalatable your views might be to others.

That's why you have neo-Nazis and white supremacists terrorizing Jewish neighbourhoods and beating up black people. That's why some deranged lunatic can legally buy a gun and shoot a great man like Martin Luther King just because he disagrees with his views. Sometimes too much freedom can be a bad thing, Venus.

Bullshit. You can never have too much freedom. Peace, prosperity and freedom. Aren't those the guiding tenets of a true democracy? But now it's brutality, intolerance and hatred. We now practice the same things we used to fight against. Where did it all go wrong?

You watch too much CNN and the BBC. Those imperialist channels will poison your mind.

Rubbish. Why are marches and demonstrations by pressure groups banned in this country? Why do people have to get permission from the police to go out onto the streets and make their grievances known?

That's unfair, Venus. There is more freedom here than in most African countries so loved by the western countries. We have opposition parties and there is a vibrant independent press.

You remember that young beggar when you picked me up from the airport?

Every country has beggars. It's not something peculiar to this country.

That's not the point I was going to make.

What *is* the point you were going to make?

That boy asked me for five billion dollars. Are you aware that at Independence in 1980 a four-bedroom house in a decent suburb costs roughly twenty thousand dollars?

Maybe. It's not a statistic that is of interest to me.

Well, it should be. If you had five billion dollars then you could buy yourself two hundred and fifty thousand houses. You could have become a bigger property mogul than Donald Trump and the Queen of England combined. Now five billion dollars just buys you a single cigarette. That's your Monopoly money for you.

Of course, there is inflation. But that is because of all these sanctions the western countries imposed on us when we took the land back.

Nonsense. All this economic misery the country is experiencing is self-inflicted. And the reason why people like you don't want to accept that fact is because you know that a self-inflicted wound is the most painful.

Okay, Venus. You have made your point, no need to rub it in. Tell me about life in America, the land of milk and honey. Tell me about the bayous of Louisiana, the jazz clubs of Baton Rouge....

Too tired to go to my own cold and lonely flat, I doze off fully clothed on the worn-out settee in the hotel room. Barely two hours later the cell-phone alarm goes off. An erotic dream is interrupted. A memory is stolen. Maria, my maid, came back last night. The villages are a war-zone, she said. Militias are beating up people, wanting to know how they voted. Sprawled across the massive bed in a pink negligee, you are snoring, smiling, sighing. You look so beautiful, so innocent and so fragile.

I tiptoe out like a ghost.

Long ago, when we were growing up, there was the old war.

Your eldest brother, Harold, was in it. He was a seventeen-year-old conscript. He didn't want to be in the army. He died in a freak accident on the Mozambican border – an excitable colleague accidentally discharging a loaded gun that just happened to be pointing at Harry. Nowadays they call it 'friendly fire', the occupational hazard of being done in by one of your own. But just like that, Harry was gone, a flame that flickered brilliantly but briefly.

Like your other dead heroes: Bob Marley, Marcus Garvey, Che Guevara, Malcolm X. Gertrude, your youngest sister, had a problem with Malcolm: How can somebody have a surname like X? she asked with that wide-eyed innocence peculiar to baffled children. But Gertrude, young as she was, had her enlightened moments. One cannot live in a perfect world, she once said. It would be too boring. Now, she too lives in the Deep South of America. She too has a green card. She too survives on Dunkin' Donuts, Wendy hamburgers, Starbucks coffee and Kentucky Fried Chicken.

You remember the one weekend Harry came back on compassionate leave after your grandmother died? He said he didn't want to be in the army any more. It was too traumatic. He couldn't even bring himself to kill a spider, Harry, and when he was young he used to faint at the sight of his own blood. He told us how his unit had raided suspected guerrilla camps on the Mozambican border. He said some of the soldiers tortured the villagers for information, burnt down the huts of suspected collaborators and raped their women. Then they spread-eagled the village headman between two trees and blew his body to pieces by firing a bazooka into his body.

Then there was your other sister, Mercy, so quiet and introspective she used to worry all of us – Mercy of the volcanic tempers and the sullen silences. Beware of the man who does not talk and the dog that does not bark, your father often chided her. In his early days your father Samson was a lay preacher, a man full of wisdom. Plagued by alcoholism, he had taken up religion as a kind of aversion therapy. He was a respected elder in the BBC – the Bible

Believing Church. He loved to tell the story of the prodigal son, how love is stronger than pride, how redemption can conquer sin. He once sat us in front of your house and told us about Adam and Eve, the serpent and the apple in the Garden of Celestial Mischief. He told us that temptation wears many hats, comes through many doors.

Be bold, be brave, my daughter. And always stand in the light when you want to speak out. You should seek strength from the Lord, not to be greater than your brother or your sister, but to fight your greatest enemy – yourself.

Because in the end our lives are nothing more than dreams, fragments, memories.

Just before you went to America we had a farewell dinner, a downtown Chinese restaurant with red paper dragons hanging from the ceiling. The place, whose speciality was sizzling dishes, came well recommended by one of our old university friends, Jerome Chitata, a veritable *bon vivant*. He later married a beautiful Swiss aid worker and went to live on the shores of Lake Geneva. It was a warm day in late May, that peculiar time when it's nearing the end of summer but still not yet quite winter.

The scent of ginger was heavy in the air. One of the waiters was a thin elderly man with crooked teeth and a mean attitude. Let him be, you said. You don't know what these people get up to when they are alone with your food in the kitchen. One of the main courses intrigued you: chicken with wooden ears. It is just chicken with seaweed, said one of the waiters, frowning discouragingly. Afterwards, we had a silly argument about black people and sports.

Yes, *that* day, *that* argument.

You had an outlandish theory: you said black women made poor gymnasts and poorer swimmers because their bums and tits are too big. Tennis is a problem too, you continued, because blacks have poor hand-to-eye co-ordination. A racist argument, the usual hackneyed stereotyping, surely you didn't expect to get away with it? But it has been proved, you insisted, that brawn and feline grace do not go hand in hand. Sport is sport, I insisted. What about Jesse Owens, Michael Jordan, Sugar Ray Robinson, Carl Lewis, Florence Griffiths-Joyner, Joe Louis, Cassius Clay? Float like a butterfly, sting like a bee?

Okay, okay… Let's talk about something else, you said. You never like losing an argument. I could have done with someone like you in my debating team at high school, tackling such weighty topics like: *Why is Africa the poorest continent when it is the richest in natural resources?* Instead, I had to make do with the mind-boggling naivety of certified ignoramuses like Imelda Gumbo and her equally daft friend Kerenzia Nzungu: Africa is poor because it's the white people who discovered everything that matters in this world – television, radio, X-rays, penicillin, aeroplanes, electricity and computers – dim-witted Kere would argue. So, you see, that is why black people will always be hewers of wood and drawers of water.

Yes, Venus, the gods will always be white and the demons will always be black.

Through your e-mails you have often accused me of being a government sympathiser, of viewing the pathetic mess our country is in through a jaundiced eye. There is nothing I can do, I have often protested. I am not the one who got the country into the mess it's in. It will take us exactly the same amount of time to get things right that it took us to get them wrong, you always argue somewhat disconsolately.

You are a prodigious dispatcher of e-mails, sending me at least twenty every week. But that's typical of you, Venus – doing things to excess or not doing them at all. You have never been a person of moderate inclinations. And yet for some strange reason your arguments become more lucid the more you drink. The more alcohol you consume, the more sense you make.

But sometimes you are just like your father Samson in his younger days, when he was a big politician and thought he had the whole world at his feet. In those days he behaved like the redneck sheriff of a small American town – vain, arrogant and extremely full of himself. If you didn't agree with him, you became his enemy. If you agreed with him, you became a dangerous rival. Lately, you have joined the bandwagon of those whose crusade is to save the earth. You have become an inveterate cyber-sage, using the technological wonders of the Internet to preach to all and sundry about how mankind has his finger poised above the self-destruct button.

You once sent me a long rambling e-mail about deadly carbon emissions, genetically modified foods, disappearing glaciers, the depletion of the ozone layer and other environmental horrors you blamed on unchecked industrialisation. Last month you told me you had joined an environmental group dedicated to saving the Siberian tiger and the snow leopard, two animals you have probably only heard about on Animal Planet.

One earth, you said, that's all we have. We take the earth's resources for granted. We use them but we never put anything back. Once we have exhausted everything on it, what do we do next? Everything in the ground is a finite resource. God is not going to make more gold, more diamonds and more platinum. God is not going to recreate animal species that we wipe out because we want to wear expensive fur coats and impress our friends with shoes made from the skins of exotic reptiles. Why should we kill an entire animal just because we want a part of its body? Back in the States I have joined a book club with like-minded citizens and once a week we discuss these issues with a view to actually making a meaningful contribution to save our planet…

Okay Venus, you win. I am a mere mortal. I have no response to your newfound worldly wisdom. Let's have a drink.

The usual?

Why not?

Waiter!

Yes?

I'll have a whisky and soda.

And I'll have a gin and tonic.

Cheers.

But time was when you used to call it something else.
Gin and talk shit.

How did our lives conjoin so perfectly? How did we merge into
the single thread of existence that has been our uniting umbilicus
since infancy? Now our circumstances are different, we have drifted
apart, followed diametrically opposed political paths. Socially, you
have gone up in the world; I have gone down. You work for an
international financial institution and I am a bank manager, dishing
out worthless billions of dollars everyday.

And yet it hasn't always been like that. When you got your first
holiday job you didn't want to tell me where you worked. You even
gave me a fictitious phone number. It belonged to a chicken abattoir
on the outskirts of town. They had never heard of you, but I insisted
you worked there. The receptionist became angry after the fifth
time I called.

There is nobody here by that name.
Are you sure?
Of course, I am sure.
She is new. Perhaps you don't know her yet.
I know everybody here. This is my father's company.
But I'm telling you…
You are blocking important calls, sir. If you keep phoning I will
call the police and report you for being a nuisance.

But that was were you actually worked. It turned out you had given
a fake name, embarrassed to be plucking broilers and road-runners
eight hours a day, six days a week. Your father was not well off
despite his ostentatious mail-order suits and the technical gadgets
that littered your living room. He lived a life of hire-purchase and
credit, of always having to borrow from Peter to pay Paul. You had
to work during the holidays to supplement your varsity fees. You
were embarrassed to be poor; you were ashamed to have nothing.
And then when I was about fourteen I contracted malaria after a
school trip to Lake Kariba and had to stay in bed for a whole week.

I remember you would visit me and sit outside our house for hours, or come in and take turns with my mother to feed me sorghum porridge, the only nutrition my enfeebled constitution could accept. I can still smell your body, the sweat of your morning's exertions and the faint mint scent of Colgate toothpaste on your breath. I can still see you holding a wooden spoon in your hand, slowly guiding it towards my unyielding mouth. The porridge is too hot; it scalds my tongue. You quickly back off, muttering apologies.

My mother takes over, her maternal instincts aroused by your *faux pas*. She expertly stirs the bowl with the spoon to cool the contents. Through a haze of an excruciating headache, I can hear the voices of the municipal workers outside. Those hard-working men, loud, rough, tough, and always laughing. They are collecting their tools from their depot near our house, ready to go to work fixing the roads. I had only been this sick once before, when I was about nine – an abscess from an impacted milk tooth. After the dentist drained out the pus from my gum I spent a whole week in bed, unable to eat, unable to talk.

Now you have a green card and all those old memories are water under the bridge.

Tuesday, April Fools' Day

The election result is expected any time soon, but there is no announcement. The electoral system seems hampered by a chronic malfunction. All normal activity is gripped by a terminal paralysis. Another day goes by, two, three, four, five. Suspicion soon replaces expectation; something sinister is definitely afoot. Rumour has it the white farmers have come back in droves. The restaurants are full of them, the hotel bars are full of them and the shopping malls are full of them. They want their land back, because the Bible says give unto Caesar what is Caesar's. Usually annoyingly vocal, the state media gives nothing away. In the absence of fact, speculation and conjecture abound. Wildly improbable text messages do the usual rounds:

There are rumours of a crushing landslide by the Opposition;

the ruling party will be lucky to get five per cent of the vote. A losing cabinet minister has been taken into custody for shooting dead a presiding officer mocking him after his humiliating defeat. A popular Vice-President has lost the safe seat she has held for twenty-eight years.

Another cabinet minister has been caught, in *flagrante delicto*, stuffing ballots into boxes to avoid certain defeat. A well-known female MP has suffered a heart attack after a thorough drubbing by the Opposition candidate. Dozens of election officers are arrested countrywide. There are accusations of attempted electoral fraud by civil servants loyal to the Opposition, of numbers being manipulated to tell the preferred story. We know figures have been cooked, both sides claim, we know ballot boxes have been tampered with.

Countless press conferences are called to allay the suspicions of an increasingly hostile media. Cornered from all sides, the electoral commission finally concedes that recounts have to be done in some marginal constituencies. Its beleaguered chairman desperately clutches at straws to justify his organisation's glaring ineptitude. At a city centre hotel, he is pursued like a common thief by a cynical press.

Days go by, people await the revelation of the stratagems used by those whose intention was to compromise the vote, to cheat the people out of their long-awaited victory. And yet more days go by. There is no smoking gun, and there is no announcement of the election result. But the writing is clearly on the wall: The ruling party has an ace up its sleeve. It is not easy to dislodge the occupants of a fortress perched on a sheer cliff. And this particular war is not over yet, not by a long shot.

This war is just starting.

The election result is finally announced. The parliamentary contest is announced constituency by constituency over a number of days in a manner stage-managed to give the impression of parity, of a tight neck-and-neck race. But the news is received with little enthusiasm, like the result of a soccer match where everybody knows the referee's impartiality has been compromised. There is a hung parliament but the presidential poll was indecisive. There will be a run-off between the two leading contenders on the 27ᵗʰ of June. There is a collective sigh of frustration. A week might be a long time in politics, but three months is an eternity.

You want to go back to America, to the Pelican State, to your private paradise on the edge of the bayou. You want to go back to your Cajun food and those balmy cruises on the Mississippi. You want to walk hand in hand with your husband admiring the Creole architecture of New Orleans' French Quarter. You want to sit in the smoky clubs of Baton Rouge and listen to the sweetly syncopated rhythms of Clifton Chernier and Rockin' Dopsie. There is no need for this run-off, you keep saying. I know our guy won outright the first time of asking. Yes, Venus, we have both seen the triumphant press conferences, heard about the wildly fluctuating margins of victory. But even the dumbest lawyer tells his client to keep his story consistent, or keep his mouth shut.

If your guy won, it was a protest vote.

So what? Every time you vote, it's a protest against something or someone. You don't really vote because you really like one candidate, but because you dislike the other guy more. An election is the only time you can legally show your displeasure.

True, true.

And if you are a politician you should win an election because people like you, not because they fear you.

That is where I beg to differ. If you are a politician you should win elections. Period.

Perhaps they should just put aside their differences and form a government of national unity.

Impossible. A mule and a bull cannot be made to pull the same plough.

Okay, okay... We might be on different sides of the political divide but we are not enemies.

I agree. I just don't want you to hold out high hopes.

I have high hopes. We all have high hopes. The time for change has finally come. How is Robin?

The stage is set. The run-off will be a duel to the bitter end, a tussle between the alpha female and the dominant male. Pictures speak louder than words. Every tree has a poster; every wall displays its political allegiance; every T-shirt displays the wearer's political preference. But we all know things will be different this time round. There is too much at stake. This time there is no need for disingenuous niceties meant to hoodwink a sceptical world. This time there are no holy principles – the rules of the new game will be made up as the game progresses.

This time there is no need to dish out tractors, buses and computers at rallies. There is no need for baby-holding photo opportunities on potholed township streets flooded with raw sewage. This time it's simply about self-preservation, and this time the ballot cannot be allowed to beat the bullet. We all know the ploy to ensure positive participation, though somewhat reprehensible, is simple and well tested: first you intimidate and dispossess, then you exterminate.

The contenders are back on the campaign trail, like hyenas and lions stalking prey in the same patch of forest. It's like a drug – the need to preach, to convince, to convert. But this time the atmosphere is different. There is fear and there is mistrust. And yet everybody agrees that if things remain the way they are, the country cannot move forward. It's a debilitating stalemate. There is need for a decisive blow, a *coup de grace*. And as the old song goes, sometimes the fate of a nation can be decided by one decision. The Man Rumoured To Have Won the first round is on an international campaign trail, savouring the taste of blood, taking his case to the highest offices. He is behaving like a hunter tracking a wounded bull elephant. But he also knows the blow he struck in the first round was glancing, not mortal. Tragically, circumspection is soon replaced by a buoyant arrogance. This time around he promises to finish off what he started. Amongst his jubilant followers there is talk of retributive justice in the New

Utopia – the International Court of Justice, punishing those who committed crimes against humanity. There is even talk of a truth and reconciliation commission.

Of course, there will be no blanket amnesty, says The Man Rumoured To Have Won the first round. All I can say is that we will look at each case on its own merits. But be assured, change is coming. Our steps were small and the journey seemed long. But now we have finally crossed the Rubicon. We stand on the bridge between a past of pain and a future of hope, between yesterday's despair and tomorrow's promise.

But forewarned is forearmed. Confusion breeds paranoia. The true warrior knows that when you have unsheathed your dagger you keep it well hidden from the enemy until the exact moment you intend to strike. This time round, The Man Rumoured To Have Lost the first round is ready. He is in a combative mood, rattling his all-conquering sabre. And every day, the bar is being raised a few more notches. Every day, the political temperature soars a few more degrees. Because winning is everything. Because nobody remembers who came second.

We are not a colony of Britain. Why should they monitor our elections? We have never monitored theirs. We can't have our former colonisers coming here and monitoring our elections. It's like inviting the ex-boyfriend of the bride to the wedding.

Talking of weddings, I remember the time you came back in 2004 for your youngest sister Gertrude's wedding to a local tycoon, a man with a rural supermarket the size of a football field. The supermarket is still there, gleaming every day in the savannah sunshine like a high-tech mausoleum. But now there is nothing on its shelves – every commodity delivered to the supermarket is sold outside by the resident army of black marketers.

The man already had two other wives. Gertrude – young, vibrant, pretty and twenty-something – was the fashionable trophy wife to take to prestigious functions, just the tonic the tycoon needed to assuage his mid-life crisis. The wedding reception was in a massive marquee garlanded with multi-coloured balloons. It was a big family reunion. Your entire clan was there. Your father, as the bride's father, made the first speech. By then he had had too much Captain Morgan rum and coke.

He stumbled onto the crowded podium, took the microphone from the deferential MC and hiccupped a slurred greeting. He made a couple of dreadful mother-in-law jokes and disparaged a few of his former comrades-in-arms who were present. It was not the time for political statements but your father gave a humorous, if somewhat wildly embellished, account of his life as a nationalist. The guests laughed because it was the polite thing to do. But the humour was underpinned by the tragic shadow of non-accomplishment we all knew followed him throughout his life like a dynastic curse. When it was time for the newly-weds to cut the cake, Gertrude was in tears. But we all knew they were not tears of joy. It was supposed to be *her* big day, not her father's.

The day before the wedding I accompanied you and your mother to an Indian bazaar on the Charter Road where you wanted to buy some hair extensions. Your head has always been adorned with other people's hair. This was a shop you had frequented since our varsity days. The fat shopkeeper said you and your mother looked like sisters. Your mother was flattered; you were appalled. Since your return, you have asked me to take you back to that same shop, but when we got there somebody said it had been closed for years. A lot of businesses have closed around here, said the man.

Meanwhile, the run-off election campaign continues unabated. Daily, the two protagonists prod each other's armoury, looking for chinks to exploit. Every man has his weakness; every man has his Achilles heel.

We are fed up of having our President demonised by those who kept us in slavery for so many years. We will never be a colony again. The western nations can go hang a thousand times. This time it's hundred percent Total War...

But every war has its casualties, Venus. You and I have been lucky; we might be the walking wounded, but we have survived. A week before the run-off election we decided that we would go and vote together on the 27th of June. We too would make our voices count. And that afterwards we would go to the Chinese restaurant with the red dragons crawling on the stained ceiling and have a huge slap-up meal to celebrate. We will celebrate whatever the outcome, we agreed, because somebody will have won and somebody will have lost.

As usual, it will be whisky and soda for me, and gin and talk shit for you.

This is your era. This is your time. The people must be empowered.

28th June 2008

You are leaving.

Came to pick you up from your hotel after lunch. The run-off was an anticlimax, but there is an all-pervasive sense of inevitability in the air, a sense of irretrievable loss. Maria, still traumatised, didn't vote and stayed indoors with Robin the whole day. The karaoke session in the building next door to the hotel is in full swing. Someone is routinely murdering *Bohemian Rhapsody*:

...Mamma mia, mamma mia, let me goh, loozh-millah, loozh-millah... Ah shee ah little shilhouette...skanda-moo-skanda-moooo-oooo-oooh...

You told me that after breakfast that morning your sister Gertrude and her husband came to say goodbye. Your father is not very well, she said; the exertions of the election campaign have finally caught up with him. He is in bed suffering from exhaustion. Gertrude's husband, Robert, gave you an assortment of presents to give your husband and family in Louisiana. You gave pot-bellied Robert a copy of your husband's latest best-selling book on dieting. *How To Lose Thirty Pounds In Thirty Days And Not End Up Looking Like A Stick Insect.*

... Galileo, Galileo, Figaro... Fandango-oooooooo... Thunder and lightning, very very frightening...

Now we are at the airport, a deserted and cold building. The atmosphere is so surreal it's like being on the set of a science fiction movie. Persistence should always be applauded and heroism should always be rewarded, but your father, Samson Erasmus Mate, is now political history. He trailed a distant third in the parliamentary constituency he contested in. But he should have known better. Was it not him who once told us that dreams are wiser than men? And yet, like his biblical namesake, he too was sweet-talked by sycophants into losing the source of his power; he too had to face the harsh reality of the non-existence of his imagined popularity.

But unlike the biblical Samson his nemesis was not a scorned woman, but the lure of riches, the mirage of an inexhaustible gravy train. And as sure as flesh becomes dust, so he too has become nothing. He will always be the permanent understudy, the fringe player who never makes the centre stage. Perhaps now he knows that politics is a profession for people who have no qualms about doing the unthinkable, people who have no conscience when it comes to defending the indefensible and people who can snuff out lives with the same disdain one snuffs out a spent candle.

Yesterday you gave me a parting gift, a video you said I should watch when I have time.

It's called 'The Madness of King George', you said. It's about what happens to a man when he has too much power. It's about how power first intoxicates, and then corrupts. Every deity has its disciples, you told me the day I picked you up from the airport; every tyrant has his worshippers. If there weren't people who thought Hitler was a messiah, there wouldn't have been a Second World War and six million Jews wouldn't have died. Power is like sex, you once said in one of your e-mails – because the more you have the more you want.

Enjoy your life on the bayou, Venus. Enjoy the soul food, the riverboat cruises, the New Orleans *Mardi Gras*, the amazing multi-level shopping malls. The American Dream might even become sweeter for you – there is a real chance there might be a black man in the White House this time next year. But I will stay here with your politically vanquished father and we will deal with the potholes, the queues, the power outages, the water shortages and the zeroes. The presidential run-off has come and gone. We never went to vote. The Man Rumoured To Have Won the first round outright pulled out of the run-off at the last minute, leaving The Man Rumoured To Have Lost the first round outright as the sole candidate. We both agreed we were not going to participate in a farce.

The rest, as the saying goes, is history.

You peck me gently on the cheek and disappear into the yawning departure hall. Five minutes after your plane takes off I drive back alone, singing the monotonous but happy tune from Room Ten.

Under my umbrella…rella rella ella ella eh eh eh eh…

2

Cities of Dust

*Evil is an emanation of human consciousness
at certain transitional points.*

(Franz Kafka, *The Zurau Aphorisms*)

Every day, you meet at the same bus stop.

You do not know her name, she has never asked you yours. She always smiles at you and as time goes by you fancy your chances. You are now thirty-eight, single and still looking. You are not getting any younger and your Casanova days are clearly past you. In your mid-twenties you amused yourself by counting the girls you had slept with. You kept their names in a little red book next to the photographs they sent you. You gave them marks based on three categories: overall beauty, performance in bed and what you called 'marriageability' – the girl's suitability as a wife. Now it's all a blur of one-night stands and forgettable flings. The past is a cold memory you have no wish to live with.

But you desperately hope the woman dressed in black you meet at the bus stop is the one.

One day the opportunity presents itself and you sit next to her on the crowded bus. It is the closest you have ever been to her. You exchange a few pleasantries. She tells you her name is

Yolanda. You can smell her cologne, the scent of her hair, her garlic breath. Because you are strangers the conversation is strained, uncomfortable, the common subjects few. She lives with her father and a younger brother but she does not tell you where. You do not ask because it is early days and you do not want to pry. You tell her you have a widowed mother at home, bedridden with chronic arthritis. You tell her you never knew your father.

'He abandoned my mother five months before I was born.'

She flinches, as if startled by the bitterness in your voice. It's almost four decades, but you have never forgiven your father. Once again, you remind yourself, it is a bad habit to tell people your problems until they tell you theirs.

You work for the same company, but because you are on different floors you rarely meet. Except at the bus stop, waiting for the company bus. She is in Accounts and you are in Human Resources. You have been to her office once, on a pretext, and she wasn't there. You guiltily scanned the paraphernalia in the room – an old family picture on the wall, Yolanda in a primary school uniform on a portrait by the desk, all dimples, gleaming braced teeth and a ponytail. On a small table, Yolanda and a female friend sit astride a bull elephant during a teenage trip to Victoria Falls, next to that picture a portrait of an aloof but handsome young man built like a rugby prop. Jealousy nags you; you wonder if this is her boyfriend. You know you have no hope in hell of competing with this finely toned superman, if indeed this is her boyfriend. You left the office before she came back, like an eavesdropper slouching away into the shadows of the night.

More than half the company's employees now use the staff bus, having been forced to park their cars because of a crippling fuel shortage. The bus is a barometer of public opinion because most of its passengers live in the high-density townships and other poorer parts of town. The political gossip is as scathing as it is relentless.

'My son's car has been parked for a full month now because he cannot get fuel. Can you believe it? He has the money but cannot get the things he wants.'

'In this country you can have all the money in the world but not find the things you want in the shops.'

'At the next election we must all vote to change things,' says one elderly man who never makes an attempt to hide his affiliation to the opposition party.

On the bus, you now regularly sit together. The closeness cements your burgeoning friendship. Now and again you exchange harmless banter. You now know she lives somewhere on the other side of town. She tells you she wears black because she recently suffered a family bereavement. You offer your belated condolences but have no wish to learn further details. You know she will tell you when she is ready.

'I used to live in Park Meadowlands,' she says. 'Then the municipality bulldozers destroyed the cottage I was renting.'

She tells you how the bulldozers destroyed the flea markets and the townships near her house, how they made thousands homeless. You heard it on radio; saw it on television. They called the bulldozers the *tsunami* – a destructive force that razed down everything in its path. There were harrowing pictures in the newspapers; little children standing in the swirling dust amidst the rubble of ruined homes. Sucking their thumbs, they looked bewildered and lost. It was a man-made disaster of incredible proportions. The city was covered in dust. The messenger at your workplace was an early victim of the *tsunami*. The day after it happened he complained about the carnage.

'Sometimes man's inhumanity to his own kind knows no bounds. They destroyed my tuck-shop and yet all I was doing was selling bread, sugar, salt and cooking oil. I was providing an invaluable service to the public.'

'Come on Enoch, your commodities were being sold at black-market prices.'

'My prices were determined by the laws of supply and demand.'

On television it is announced that the *tsunami* is to spread countrywide. The police spokesman on the news says it is only the beginning. This is not a game, he warns those entertaining 'funny ideas'.

'If you corner an injured lion it will maul you.'

Friday morning.

The bus is full today because more people have parked their cars at home. The country is completely dry; the only fuel available is on the black market and selling at ten times the pump price. As usual, you sit next to Yolanda. For the first time she tells you she has a son.

'His name is Ephraim,' she says. 'He is two.'

She scrimmages through her handbag and brings out a small shiny wallet. She hands you a colour photograph. The boy looks like the aloof but handsome young man built like a rugby prop whose photograph you saw in Yolanda's office. Same bushy brows, same toothy grin and the same cleft chin. It's your chance to pry.

'He doesn't look like you.'

'No. He looks like his father,' she says, and then abruptly puts the photograph back in her handbag. She looks away and clasps her hands. A man behind you is recounting how he went to his house the previous day and found himself a *tsunami* victim.

'The bulldozers were merciless. There was nothing left. Nothing.'

On your way back from the work that day there is a protest in the city centre. It's a cold, grey day. The winter sun slips in and out of the clouds, a vertiginous blue light. From your elevated seat on the bus you can see the marchers waving their banners. Vendors attracted by the huge crowds line the street displaying their wares. Bananas, sweets, oranges, single cigarettes. Where large numbers congregate, there is good business. There's a jovial, carnival atmosphere. The crowd is made up of men, women and children.

'Down with poverty!' they yell in one resounding wall of sound.

For a while, you watch the small group of women marching

alongside the bus. At the front of the marchers – her hair tousled, her feet bare – is a lone white woman. *Women of Zimbabwe Unite* – reads the banner she holds above her head. *WOZA*, echo the inscriptions on the other marchers' T-shirts – a belligerent acronym that invokes images of an imminent proletarian insurrection. These women want freedom, they want free speech and they want to reclaim the lost dignity of their once great nation.

The marchers are in a jovial mood until the riot police arrive. The black-booted policemen leap from their trucks, baying the way hounds do when they have cornered a fox in a copse. These men have been conditioned to subscribe to the creed that the only way to ensure peace is through violence. A confrontation is imminent; the prelude is a tidal wave of obscenities and insults. The women, grim-faced, outnumbered and outgunned, continue their march in silence. But before long the batons are out. Some of the riot police start chanting.

'*Zimbabwe ndeyeropa, baba… Zimbabwe ndeyeropa, baba…*'

The women scream, shout, wail, and then wilt under the merciless onslaught. The violence is over as quickly as it began. Torn banners and shoes lie scattered on the tarmac, a forlorn reminder of the power of brute force. A child that has been separated from its mother during the mayhem stands crying on the pavement. Those marchers unable to get away are bundled into the police trucks, bloodied, battered but unbowed. As the trucks drive away a brave passer-by shouts encouragement, raising his fists into the air in solidarity. With that single poignant gesture, the women's resolute defiance has been transformed from a position of hopelessness into a heroic last stand.

But the WOZA women should have known better – when a castle's battlements are under siege, compliance and order must be preserved at all costs. Sometimes, you defend best by attacking. Fortitude has its limits, and the courageous aren't always victorious. It is an accepted way of life here that those against the *status quo* will always be arrested. But to conquer is not to convince; silencing your opponents is a futile deterrent. Capital punishment has never stopped murderers, and cutting of a man's hands has never stopped other thieves from stealing.

It is not in your interests to do or say anything. You are safe where you are, at the back of the bus. The riot police manage to clear the street. The bus moves on. When Yolanda nears her stop she tells you she had a stepsister who died in a train disaster in South Africa. There was a symbolic funeral because there was nothing left to bury.

'That's why I wear black. I am still in mourning.'

'I'm sorry to hear that.'

The bus stops and half a dozen people get ready to dismount. Yolanda stands up and adjusts her coat.

'By the way, do you know anybody who works at the British Embassy?'

'No. Why?'

'I want to apply for British visas for myself and Ephraim.'

'You want to go to England?'

'Maybe.'

On Saturday afternoon you accompanied her to a secret meeting at a venue in the city centre. On the way she tells you her late sister's name was Temptation. It is your first political meeting. The hall is full of young black men with short haircuts and smart suits, the brash newcomers of politics – what a relative of yours aligned to the ruling party disparagingly calls 'sell-outs'. Speaker after speaker speaks of a bright new future, a new beginning. It is the first time you have heard the government denounced by so many.

'We are powerless not because we are few, but because we fear. We are our own worst enemy.'

During the coffee and biscuit intermission, you meet one of the speakers in the corridor outside and share in the optimism of the newly converted. He is a well-known student activist, one of the rising stars of the opposition. Loud and arrogant, he swaggers with astonishing over-confidence. When he speaks you listen intently.

'The ruling party is in disarray and the opposition is fragmented. We have to chart a new course forward. Now is the time to create a Third Force.'

Afterwards there are prayers for victims of political violence and when you leave you feel reborn, sanctified. You can now walk tall, your soul cleansed, your conscience purified. The idea of a Third Force excites you, but somehow, deep down, you know it will never be; many before you have been to this same bridge and never been able to cross it.

It is a cold Monday morning.

Last night there was a live international football match on television, your team against one from West Africa. You knew you had no chance. The West Africans defenders look like mastodons; your country's entire population was pinning its hopes on a player whose best days were well and truly behind him. The bus judders along the busy street, burdened by its usual load of sleepy bodies.

Yolanda is not on the bus. The people on the seat in front of you are discussing the football match. You learn that the West African mastodons won four-nil. That does not surprise you. One of the speakers blames the pre-match training facilities, the match officials, the national coach and all the players. That does not surprise you either. The front pages of the newspaper say the *tsunami* has moved to the posh northern suburbs. The news is greeted with barbed comments from the back rows of the bus.

'Its just a political gimmick, they will not destroy anything there.'

'What makes you so sure?'

'That's where most of them live. You think they can be stupid enough to destroy their own properties?'

'And the people in the posh suburbs know the law, unlike the poor lodgers whose shacks were destroyed in the townships.'

In the northern suburbs the *tsunami* finally runs out of steam. A wealthy white man is known to have built a complex of shops and offices without the necessary statutory approvals. There are suggestions that palms were greased for the powers that be to turn a blind eye to the massive development. For once the passengers on the company bus echo the same sentiments.

'They have to destroy the white man's shopping centre, just like they destroyed the townships.'

'Otherwise it's one law for the rich and one law for the poor.'

'Or worse still, it's one law for whites and one law for us blacks.'

'Everybody knows people were bribed. That white man is a well-known crook.'

Yolanda.

You have not seen her for a few days now – not on the bus, not at the bus stop and not at the staff canteen. You have no idea where she is, but it's too early to press the panic button. You have more pressing issues to attend to. Your mother's condition has deteriorated. She has become incontinent, absent-minded and forgetful. Sometimes she cannot remember your name. She needs constant attention. You have borrowed money and hired a maid who comes in the mornings only. She cleans your mother's room, cooks her some food and does the washing. You don't know what to do. You cannot afford to put her on medical aid, all you can do now is wait and hope for the best. The petrol queues are getting longer by the day. Cars line up bumper to bumper, sometimes stretching around entire blocks.

Yolanda.

You have not seen her for a full week; now you really are getting anxious. A discreet inquiry with one of her work-mates has yielded an unpalatable possibility.

'I think she went to England. The father of her son lives there.'

You suddenly feel betrayed; there is burning anger in your chest. But then there was never anything between the two of you. You will get over her. Grief is itself a medicine, tears wash away bitter sorrows and the passage of time is a palliative that heals painful memories.

There is another political meeting at a city centre hotel. You once accompanied Yolanda to the same place for a talk by a militant student activist. But it will be a good starting point to make more enquiries about her. As usual, the place is packed to the rafters. Outside, cars are double-parked on the narrow streets. You wonder where all these people are getting fuel. Today the main speaker is a former government minister. Within minutes the man is in full stride:

'Ladies and gentlemen, we stand on the verge of a new beginning. History has shown that there are no invincible armies, and the glory of great men must always be measured against the means they have used to obtain it.'

Afterwards there is tea and biscuits in the hotel lobby. The former minister is holding court in a corner. Like most men of his kind, he has a magnetic appeal that is irresistible to the gullible. A coterie of hangers-on surrounds him, savouring his every word. The student activist from the previous meeting introduces you. You wince when the former minister addresses you as 'comrade'.

'The regime is on its last legs,' he says, 'but it's not finished yet. As the Spanish say – the body of the beast might have been flayed, but there is a good deal of flesh still left in the tail.'

He has always had a way with words, the former minister. But so did Hitler, and so did Judas. He was once powerful, this man, introducing a spate of draconian laws that set his country's human rights record back a whole century. 'An enigma', one political commentator once called him. And, as with most enigmas, he enjoyed the impenetrable mystique this incongruous status bestowed upon him and became godlike in his arrogance; but like most mortals, he too had his Achilles heel, the inherent defect that brings down kings and paupers alike. There is no doubt in your mind that the so-called Third Force will be another juggernaut of confusion, another stillborn dragon.

One of your country's poets once wrote that history writes itself on leaves and blank spaces. But you know that a new future cannot be born out of a past that is not completely dead. And you also know that history, any history, does not write itself on blank minds.

3

Kaffir Corn

Nothing in the affairs of men is worthy of great anxiety.
(Plato, *Republic*)

25th December 2002

After the Christmas lunch there isn't really much to do. It's hot, and swarms of flies are buzzing over the leftover food. My father suggests that we all go for a drive to the new farm he has just been given by the government. It's a suggestion that receives a lukewarm response from everybody. The road is bumpy and people's stomachs are full of turkey. But there isn't really much to do, so we all decide to go to the farm. Besides, my mother says, the fresh air will do us all the world of good. It is also another opportunity for my father to test his brand-new VW Microbus, which he says will get us there in no time. As we leave the house we notice some of the local gardeners are already sprawled on the sides of the roads, dead drunk. My grandmother says they must have drunk *kachasu*.

'It's the only drink I know that can make grown men behave so stupidly,' she says.

The car hit the dog as we approached the traffic lights at the shopping centre. In an effort to avoid hitting the dog my father applied the brakes suddenly but it was too late. The dog, a brown mongrel with a white stripe across its muzzle, was thrown into the air and ended up on its back. It lay on the road, its limbs twitching violently. There was blood gushing out of its mouth and nostrils. There was nothing anybody could do, so we just left it there, a sad creature bleeding to a slow death in the dust.

The new farm my father was recently allocated by the government as part of the land reform programme is about two hundred and eighty kilometres to the west of the city. The white farmer, Mr Allan Bradford, wouldn't budge at first, so my father had to go to the farm with some of his hefty relatives and force the man out. The incident was widely reported in the press and made father something of a minor celebrity. That was his fifteen minutes of fame. He loved the attention and at weddings and funerals often amused people by retelling the story of how he had kicked out the stubborn Bradford from Pangolin Farm.

Father knew the government official responsible for the farm allocations in the province of his choice – an old comrade from the embryonic days of the 'Struggle' – and was given a list of half a dozen farms to choose from. His first preference was New Jacaranda Estate, a thriving citrus concern about seventy miles out of town. The estate provided the country with half its oranges. The other half earned foreign currency in several European Union countries. But his friend who did the allocations told him too many ruling party *chefs* were after the same farm and warned my father that he might find himself in a bruising tug-of-war. Father had settled for Pangolin Farm because of its rich cotton soil and temperate climate.

My father is very excited by the idea of being a New Farmer. He was born and brought up in the city and says he cannot wait to live in a place where everyday he can feel and taste the fresh air of the great outdoors. He says he cannot wait to be part of Nature. He spent the whole of last month proudly showing all his friends and relatives the offer letter from the Ministry that proclaimed him the new owner of Pangolin Farm. He says once he realises the grand plans he has for the farm, poverty will be a thing of the past for us.

My father has always entertained fantastic money-making schemes that he assures us will one day make him rich beyond the dreams of avarice. Every time he reads in the newspaper of a massive fraud committed by some junior bank teller he whistles and shakes his head in admiration. He has always had a soft spot for daring criminals. When I was young he used to read 'True Detective' and told us about the Great Train Robbery of England. And even after a few stiff Scotches he can still reel off the names of the villains involved, men who collectively boasted a vast portfolio of petty crime – Bruce Reynolds, Tommy Wisbey, Roy Jones, Ronald Biggs, Charlie Wilson, Gordon Goody, Jimmy White.

He also admires Aidan Diggeden, a local small-time thief and legendary jail-breaker who eventually got deported to England, his country of origin, after the Justice Minister, like Pontius Pilate when Jesus was finally brought to him, finally washed his hands of the evasive crook. Father told us that while incarcerated in a Bulawayo prison, Diggeden would periodically break out to commit daring robberies. Afterwards, he would break back into prison and stash the proceeds of his crimes in his cell. Later on, during a five-year hiatus between jailbreaks, Diggeden even became a national trampoline champion.

Although he is not poor, my father is not exactly rich either. He says he would like to make enough money to buy a house in the northern suburbs where some of his rich friends live, something with a chip-tile pool, Jacuzzi, tennis court and other state-of-the-art modern conveniences that passed him by during the time he was exiled in Tanzania, playing his part in the 'Struggle'. Whenever my father talks about the 'Struggle' he hushes his voice, like a trespasser walking through a hallowed shrine. He often tells us how, when he was at the University of Rhodesia, he fought the injustices enshrined in a system that determined a person's worth on the basis of colour. But he also admits it was never going to be easy to be an equal citizen in an unequal society.

There is nothing wrong with the house we live in now, but

my father says it's in a 'wrong area' – Waterfalls. He has always considered the southern part of the city – with its askew tin-roofed houses and huge unkempt gardens – cheap and tacky. He also says he would like to change my mother's car, which he says has outlived its legitimate lifespan. The car is always breaking down and my mother now doesn't use it much, except to go the supermarket or to pick Eric from school. My father is always saying how wealthy so-and-so is, how the previous day so-and-so had bought such-and-such a car, and how so-and-so and his family went to such-and-such an exotic resort for holiday, and how so-and-so's daughter or son went to such-and-such a ridiculously expensive school. But he has not given up yet; he still feels his time is yet to come. Maybe Pangolin Farm will do the trick.

The farm was originally called Coomb Farm, but when it was gazetted it became Pangolin Farm. Father says it's because there have been several of these ugly and scaly animals found on the farm. Pangolins are shy and rarely seen, and if you come across one it is considered a good omen. Although the meat is supposed to be tasty nobody is allowed to kill pangolins. If you find one on your land you have to call the people from the Department of Parks and Wildlife. In the old days all the pangolins captured by villagers were given to chiefs because, according to African tradition, they are the only ones allowed to eat them. Considering how ugly pangolins are, I always felt sorry for the chiefs.

Apart from my parents, my grandmother and her younger sister are also in the car. My grandmother, Rona, is eighty-something and hard of hearing. When you talk to her you have to cup your mouth in your hands and shout, even if you are sitting right next to her. Her sister Lydia is considerably younger, but equally stone-deaf. As far as I recall, Lydia has lived wherever her sister Rona has lived. For many years, aunt Lydia worked for a white family in Highlands, George and Lily Sinclair. My father told me that Mrs Sinclair was always having rows with her husband, a senior policeman in the colonial government. She didn't like the way her husband treated the African servants and constantly accused him of having a 'plantation mentality'.

Then there is my uncle Reggie and his wife aunt Monica. Aunt Monica is coloured and grew up in St. Martins. She says 'graze' when she means food, and when she wants you to tell her something she says 'so, tune us'. Sitting at the back are my younger brother Eric and myself. Somewhere amongst the boxes of paper serviettes and plastic cartons of packed lunches and fruit behind us is our pet poodle, Franco. The conversation soon turns to farming, with uncle Reggie and aunt Monica listening very intently because they are soon to be the beneficiaries of a sizable tract of farmland to the south of the country. Like my father, uncle Reggie is also a 'born location' who has never lived in the countryside.

'I hope my son Reggie is not going to be one of these so-called cell-phone farmers,' says my grandmother jokingly and everybody laughs.

'We don't know anything about farming, so we will employ a good farm manager,' says aunt Monica defensively.

And the employment of a farm manager is the main reason for our trip to Pangolin Farm. Along the way to the farm we see a lot of new settlements on the sides of the road. There are people working in the fields, men in bright overalls and gumboots and women with infants strapped on their backs. The odd tractor rumbles across the burning horizon, spewing withered maize stalks and clouds of dust into the sky. It is a scene of pastoral industriousness that brings a wistful tear to my grandmother's eye. All around these people are their new habitations – small dwellings made of rammed earth, enormous brick structures roofed with asbestos sheets and even some double-story houses with elaborate architectural designs. Father says the dwellings belong to people who have invaded the farms formerly owned by Europeans.

'It's chaotic,' he says. 'These people should wait to be properly allocated land by the government like we have done, not just to go wherever they feel like and take over. This sort of thing gives us a bad image, internationally.'

'These people', as father calls them, have taken over the farms because they have found the whole process of waiting for offer letters from the Ministry lengthy and cumbersome. Land is what they fought for, they argue, and it seems logical to them that since it is now available they should help themselves to it. Although the government has forbidden these unsanctioned farm takeovers a groundswell of non-compliance is surging like a veldt-fire throughout the countryside. The invaders put forward a very simple argument for their unilateral actions: in the abundance of water only the fool is thirsty.

We drive along for about twenty-five kilometres through lush and evergreen meadowlands before father soon resumes his favourite topic, Pangolin Farm, the pot of gold at the end of his rainbow.

'The arable part of the farm is over two hundred hectares,' he says proudly, emphasising the word 'hundred'.

'I intend to put a quarter of that under paprika. Paprika brings in real money… American dollars and British sterling,' he adds with a self-congratulatory smugness.

This doesn't make sense to my nine-year old brother Eric, who is sitting at the back of the car with me. He wants to know how big two hundred hectares really is. For Eric, size, like distance, is relative. He cannot visualise anything beyond the scale of the miniature furniture in his Grade Four classroom.

'Just think of thirty car parks next to each other,' says my mother, trying to make it easy for Eric.

'Yes, but which car park? Westgate? Avondale? Fife Avenue? Sam Levy's Village?'

Uncle Reggie tries a different analogy.

'Two hundred hectares is five hundred acres, Eric.'

'But what's an acre?'

'Your house in Waterfalls is on one acre. Now just think of five hundred houses just like yours standing next to each other. That's how big Pangolin Farm is.'

'Five hundred houses only?'

I am beginning to get annoyed by Eric's puerile intransigence. It is the same attitude he displays when trying not to do his homework because he wants to finish watching 'Dexter's Lab' on Cartoon Network.

'Eric, you know the giant sports stadium where the national soccer team plays its games?'

Uncle Reggie had once taken us to the giant stadium to watch the national team being soundly drubbed by the Congolese, an experience that had left my soccer-mad uncle traumatised for days.

'Yes.'

'Well, imagine fifty of those stadiums next to each other. That's two hundred hectares for you.'

'Including all those car parks?'

'Yes, including all those car parks.'

'And all those outside toilets?'

'And all those outside toilets.'

Eric says nothing. But I can see from the stupefied expression on his face that he has finally got the point.

After travelling for about two and half hours we turn off the main road and drive down a narrow dirt road for another thirteen kilometres. We are now on Pangolin Farm, heading for the main homestead up on a flat granite ridge. As soon as the car gets onto the bumpy gravel it becomes quite apparent that despite father's earlier assertions about the vehicle's sturdy chassis, the VW Microbus is not the ideal vehicle for the rough terrain of Pangolin Farm. All of us hang on to the seat in front of us, bobbing and rocking until father finally heeds mother's protestations and slows the vehicle down to a reasonable pace.

'You should have bought a proper four-by-four,' says uncle Reggie when he had got his breath back.

'Or a Jeep Cherokee,' echoes aunt Monica. 'Those Cherokees are nice. That's what we are getting when we get our new farm.'

Father remains determinedly silent. He never likes it when people criticise his judgments. The journey, to the most westerly part of Mashonaland West province, should really have taken about two hours, but we had to patiently contend with my mother's usual admonitions whenever she thinks father is speeding or about to overtake injudiciously, and my grandmother's whispered but frequent requests for lengthy roadside 'recesses'.

Before we left the house my grandmother and her sister Lydia shared about a dozen cups of tea between them. That is all they ever do at the house, sit outside on the veranda and have lots of tea and buttered bread. Ever since her husband died my grandmother and her sister have shared an uneventful, monastic existence. But the truth is my grandmother just wants the recess to go outside and stretch her legs and breathe some fresh air. She does not like being inside cars. She says the fuel fumes give her heartburn.

The entrance to the Pangolin Farm homestead is a narrow dirt road sandwiched between two huge granite boulders. Immediately to our left a huge field lies fallow, the tilled top soil black and moist. A feverish excitement grips me; maybe that's where my father's foreign currency earning paprika project is going.

'What's that?' says Eric, pointing excitedly to hazy and lumpy shapes in the distance.

'It's cattle,' says my grandmother, clicking her tongue disparagingly. Then she looks at my mother.

'Eunice, you see how your city children don't even know what the animal that gives them burgers and mince meat looks like? Hmm? *Tsk... tsk...*'

Eric, visibly crestfallen, goes quiet for the rest of the journey. As we drive into the farm father points out the spot where his legendary standoff with the inflexible Mr Allan Bradford took place, exactly a year ago to the day.

'Bradford stood there with some of his uneducated farm labourers who were armed with knobkerries and sticks and said I could not drive in.'

'He said *you* could not drive into the farm?

'Yes, he said *I* could not drive into the farm.'

'The farm that the government had given *you*?'

'The farm that the government had given *me*.'

'Then what did you do?'

My mother is asking the leading questions not out of curiosity, but out of courtesy. She knows my father expects her to ask those questions. All of us have heard the story before, but this time it is being told for the benefit of uncle Reggie and aunt Monica, who have recently come back from Cape Town where they both worked for three years. The story of my father's encounter with the white farmer changes with each re-telling, this time we just don't know which particular details will be embellished and which ones omitted.

It all depends on his overall mood and the type of audience. One version, which he favours to recount at political gatherings, has him punching the six-foot fifteen-stone Allan Bradford in the face and calling him unmentionable things while the frightened African labourers flee in all directions. But with us children and two of his mothers-in-law in the car, he opts for the sanitised well-trodden version.

'He said I wanted to take over the farm so I could run it down by growing Kaffir corn.'

'He said that!'

'He said that.'

'To your face?'

'To my face.'

'And then what did you do?'

'Yes, Henry,' says aunt Monica, hunching forward in her seat with feverish anticipation. *'Tune us.'*

This is father's favourite part of the story, the bit with the real action. He slows the car down and then lets out a grunt of scornful derision, an arrogant smirk unashamedly playing on his face.

'I told Bradford not to talk to a man of my stature like that. "You can say such things to your uneducated farm labourers, but not to me," I told him. Then I looked him straight in the face and said, "I am one of the people you Boers called terrorists before Independence, and I don't accept nonsense." I also told him that with his attitude, he was lucky to still be in the country. "We finished with your type of white man in 1980," I told him.'

'*Ehe*,' said my mother.

'Good,' said aunt Monica.

'That's what they like to be told,' echoed uncle Reggie.

As the hillock upon which the homestead sat loomed on the hazy horizon my grandmother asked for another 'recess'. My mother said we were almost near the main homestead. Could she just wait for five more minutes and then use the proper sanitary facilities that were in the house?

The seven men to be interviewed for the vacant farm manager's job were already waiting for us when we reached the imposing homestead. They stood chatting uneasily in the deep shade of an adjacent storage shed, clutching briefcases or colourful paper folders. Every so often they would warily size each other up, the way boxers do before the bell for the first round. The house had a tiled roof and a pea-shaped swimming pool in front of the living room veranda. The pool's water was black and oily, and an unseen bullfrog chimed a melancholic refrain from a clump of lilies floating in the pool's deep end. Parts of the house seemed to have been recently vandalised; strips of ceiling hung from fractured roof rafters and the glass had been broken in some of the windows. I wondered whether Mr Bradford had been responsible for all that damage. But it was obvious that some time in the dark mists of memory, this was once a house that had seen prosperous times.

While all of us stood there marvelling at the sheer grandeur of the homestead, father collected the men's papers and studied them as he walked to an office building adjacent to the house. We sat on the veranda, away from the scorching sun, and my mother unwrapped the bacon and egg sandwiches she had prepared as mid-afternoon snacks. It was surprising how the bumpy journey seemed to have made everybody hungry. Eric and Franco were soon running around the garden, excitedly exploring their new surroundings as small boys and small dogs are wont to. My grandmother sat rocking in a garden chair, staring open-mouthed at the huge house. It seemed her desire to relieve her bladder had been suddenly outweighed by the need to satisfy her child-like curiosity.

'The white people lived well,' was her only comment.

One by one, the prospective farm managers would go into the office where father sat, spend a few minutes being interviewed and then emerge with different expressions on their faces. The last man to be interviewed was the one who got the job. He was a stoutly built, middle-aged man with the stooping gait of an orang-utan, and as he came out he vigorously shook all our hands and said he was looking forward to working on Pangolin Farm now that it was under a black man. He said he had been the assistant farm manager under Mr Bradford and being appointed the new farm manager was a childhood dream that had come true. He said he had worked on Pangolin Farm all his life and knew the black cotton soil like the back of his hand.

'This is the best soil for farming,' he said; 'as long as there is rain, harvests here are always bountiful.'

We sat with him on the veranda of the living room and my mother offered him some of the bacon and egg sandwiches. He said he didn't eat pork because he was a member of the Apostolic Faith. He didn't like eggs very much either, but gave no reason for this particular aversion. My mother offered him some fruit, which he accepted. When he was leaving he thanked my father for the umpteenth time and repeated the ritual of vigorously shaking all our hands, clasping mine so hard it felt as if the bones would snap.

'I have to leave now. These other men said they would be here at four o'clock,' he told my father.

'Which other men?'

'I don't know them. They refused to give me their names. They were here again last week. They brought some people to look at the irrigation pipes that were sabotaged by Mr Bradford.'

After it became apparent that his departure was inevitable, Mr Bradford had embarked on a campaign of deliberately sabotaging every piece of equipment.A JCB front-loader had pushed an entire compost heap into a well, rendering the water undrinkable. Father didn't know what to make of what his new manager was saying, but he said since it was almost four o'clock there was no harm in waiting for the unknown visitors.

At about ten past four a pair of battered Land Rovers pulled up in front of the homestead. There were four men in each vehicle, all uniformly clad in the same bright overalls worn by the people we had earlier seen working the fields along the main road. They shook our hands, exchanged the usual pleasantries, and then sat down with us on the veranda. They declined my mother's offer of sharing our bacon and egg sandwiches. They seemed impatient. The driver of one of the trucks introduced himself.

'I am Conrad Mafuta, chairman of the Haka Farm Resettlement Committee.'

'I am Henry Gwanhure, these people are my family and I am the owner of this farm,' said my father.

'No, Mr Gwanhure. This is our farm,' said Mr Mafuta, his voice firm but polite.

'We are the War Vets who chased away Bradford,' said one of Mr Gwanhure's colleagues.

'Surely, there must be some mistake...'

'There is no mistake. This is the land of Chief Haka, Mr Gwanhure. We are his descendants and this is our ancestral land.'

'Mr Mafuta, I have a letter from the Ministry giving me ownership of this farm. Maybe you would like to read it?'

Mr Mafuta waved his hand and gave my father a weak smile.

'You are not the first person to come here with a letter from the Ministry, Mr Gwanhure. There have been other people before you. Four, five, six... We have lost count. This land was taken from Chief Haka by force in 1896, during the First Chimurenga. As far as we know, he never sold it to anyone. My grandfather

Chauruma Mafuta was the fourth son of Chief Haka. This is the land of my ancestors, Mr Gwanhure. We are the ones who chased away Bradford from this land. Where were those people who gave you the letter when Bradford was setting his dogs on us? Where were they when Bradford's father burnt our parents' huts and destroyed their livestock in 1956? Where were they when Bradford's grandfather hanged my grandfather Chauruma Mafuta for fighting the British in 1897? We are fed up with you people from the towns coming to reap where you did not sow. You can take your letter back to the people who gave it to you and tell them that the Haka people have taken back their land and will not be moved again, come what may.'

On the drive back to the city everybody is quiet. Even my grandmother doesn't ask for her usual 'recess'. In the soft glow of a December sunset the hills squatting on the distant horizon seem to be covered in gold dust. We can all sense my father's anger and frustration at the unexpected turn of events. I have only ever seen him this moody when he talks about the legion of 'sell-outs' who jumped ship during the 'Struggle'. In the end, Mr Mafuta and his equally belligerent colleagues had threatened to go and bring reinforcements from the fields along the main road if we didn't leave the farm immediately. Under the circumstances, leaving had seemed the most prudent action to take. What had particularly annoyed my father were Mr Mafuta's parting words as we drove away from the house. He had accused my father of being a *muchekadzafa*.

As we drove past the stone lions either side of the imposing gate to the homestead my grandmother explained to aunt Monica, whose command of the vernacular was not very good, what the word meant.

'It means a lazy person who benefits from somebody else's hard work, like a hunter in the habit of finishing off animals already injured by another hunter. That's a *muchekadzafa*.'

The car drove on for half an hour while we all sat in complete silence.

'Do you think Mr Mafuta and his friends are real War Vets?' asked aunt Monica, in an obvious attempt to break the painful silence.

'I mean… did those guys really fight in the war? They looked a bit on the young side for me. Mafuta himself looks about thirty. That means when the war finished in 1979 he must have been about five.'

'That man is never a War Vet,' scoffed my mother, without offering any explanation to support this bold statement. My mother always jumped at the opportunity to support my father who sometimes accused her, whenever they strongly disagreed on some political issue, of sounding like a member of the Opposition.

'These are the people I told you about, the ones who are just taking over farms that they have not been given,' said my father finally.

'Maybe, it really is their land,' said my grandmother. 'It's true that a lot of people were chased off their land by the whites.'

Mother quickly steered the conversation back to her preferred path. Like my father, grandmother was a die-hard adherent of old school 'Struggle' politics. My mother looked at her husband.

'So, what are you going to do?'

'It's very simple, really. I have an offer letter. It's stamped, dated and signed by the relevant authorities. After the Christmas holiday I will go to the Ministry and I can assure you, stern action will be taken. Mr Mafuta and his friends will be off the farm in no time. We really have to put an end to this chaos.'

'Was that man telling the truth when he said they chased Bradford off the farm? This was aunt Monica.

'I am the one who chased away Bradford from Pangolin Farm. It was in all the newspapers. It was even on the television news.'

'*Ehe,*' echoed my grandmother.

It is early evening when we drive into the outskirts of town. My grandmother and her sister Lydia are dozing softly in their seats. Aunt Monica is reading a well-thumbed fashion magazine and Eric is just staring out of the window, lost in secret thoughts. But I can tell he is still sore at being told off by grandmother for failing to recognise a herd of cattle. When the car stops by the traffic lights at the shopping centre near our house Franco, our pet poodle, sits upright on my lap. He stares out of the window, whimpering plaintively.

The mongrel with the white strip across its muzzle my father hit with the car earlier that day has been moved to the side of the road. The blood on the road, which had been a startling scarlet that time, has now congealed to a leathery crimson mass. The dead dog lies still in the dust, flies buzzing around its gaping mouth. An overcrowded commuter omnibus, dangerously overtaking us on the left, runs over the dead dog's stiff hind legs.

'*Muchekadzafa*,' says Eric glumly, the first word he has uttered in over four hours.

'*Ehe*,' agrees my grandmother.

4

A Wasted Land

In times of war, the law falls silent ...
(Cicero)

Uncle Nicholas came back from England after the war in January 1981. He spent the entire fourteen hours that the journey lasted trussed up in a straitjacket, between two burly cabin crew. On arrival at the airport he was met by a four-car police escort and taken straight to the psychiatric unit at Harare Hospital. For his waiting relatives, most of whom had not seen him for twenty-five years, it was a traumatic homecoming.

I had been born in his absence and only knew him from a sepia-edged black and white photograph he had sent to my father on his arrival. It was of him and a friend standing ankle-deep in fresh snow with pigeons perched on their heads and arms. Throughout most of my childhood my memory of him consisted of that hazy, unsatisfactory likeness that was twenty years out of date. Yet it told me nothing about his behavioural quirks: how he talked, how he walked, how he laughed – whether he drank or smoked. In short, I could not visualise the whole without knowing its parts.

When he killed himself in March 1981 by cutting his wrists, all I was left with were confused memories of weekly visits to the hospital bed of a heavily drugged and pathetic old man, who soiled himself and had to be chained to the bedposts to curtail the intermittent orgies of self-inflicted violence provoked by deep bouts of melancholy. It was an inescapable yet poignant irony that he had gone overseas to better himself, not to come back in disgrace to swell the ranks of burned-out, unhinged 'been-tos' with minds contaminated by too much learning.

For the last eight years of his self-imposed exile he had stopped writing altogether. My father wrote to him regularly but in the end stopped because all his letters came back saying there was no such person known at that address. Nobody knew what uncle Nicholas was doing or where he was doing it. Eventually, it seemed, nobody cared much. We knew he was still alive because he sent the occasional Christmas card, and sometimes we went to the post office to collect boxes of second-hand clothes he bought at street markets. When my paternal grandmother died he did not know about it until my father sent a message with a woman who had won a British Council scholarship to study pharmacy at the same college that was uncle Nicholas's last known abode.

Up to this day, nobody knows why he went mad, or why in the end he thought it necessary to take his own life. His madness gradually got worse and in the end, out of sheer desperation, father had to take him out of the hospital and put him into the care of a traditional healer. At night he hardly slept, consumed as he was by terrifying nightmares in which he was pursued by the demons that had taken up residence in his unhinged mind and so corrupted his language that all he was capable of was a dialect of carnal profanities. He slept a lot, ate very little and soon managed to reduce himself to a gaunt mass of bones.

The traditional healer left one rainy night and never came back.

Later on, we were to learn – through unsubstantiated rumour, naturally – that after completing his studies he had moved on to Manchester, taken an English wife, and fathered several children. The story was all the more incredible because in Rhodesia he was still married to my aunt Emily, with whom he had three grown-up children. Another rumour, from a different source, said he had subsequently spent six years in a British jail for wife-battery and child-abuse. This seemed to explain his long silence in the seventies. When he came out his wife had the marriage annulled on the grounds of his cruelty. She sought a court order that prevented him from seeing his own children. He foolishly threatened to kill her and was promptly deported. Those who had nothing to do other than speculate about the reasons for his madness identified the woman's callousness as the pebble that dislodged the avalanche of derangement that finally overwhelmed him.

Sometimes I would look at that old black and white photograph, which my father had relegated from pride of place in the living room to the back of his bedroom door, and wonder how such a brilliant and gifted man could have been capable of the cruelties that were alleged of him. And yet it is quite often said that the calmest features hide the most scheming minds. In the early years my father made sure everybody in the street and beyond knew that his young brother Nicholas Musoni – the precociously gifted former herd-boy who wrote prize-winning essays on the Pioneer Column and the Great Trek and the Battle of Blood River – was studying clinical pharmacology at the University of London; that when he completed his doctorate he would be the first indigenous black Rhodesian to hold such a qualification. On most occasions the boast was met by politely bemused blank stares: Pharmacology? Was it something to do with farming, perhaps…? Father's simplified explanation was to tell people that uncle Nicholas was learning how to make Cafenol and Disprin.

Yes, uncle Nicholas, even though he might not have known it himself, was a man on the verge of creating momentous history.

But in the days after uncle Nicholas's death and before his own suicide my father rarely talked about him. When he did he no longer referred to him as my 'kid brother' but as 'that unfortunate brother of mine'. It was almost as if he felt that by propagating this subtle but un-brotherly denunciation he could distance himself from the accusatory fingers that were looking for somewhere to point.

He after all had been the instigator of uncle Nicholas's decision to study abroad. In truth, there had been nowhere for him to go after he had been expelled from the University of Rhodesia for his political activities. The letters he wrote in his first year abroad were all opened by the Special Branch before they were delivered, usually a good month from the date of the postmark. Once, we even got a Christmas card from him a week before Easter.

Despite the fact that he was thousands of miles away in England, uncle Nicholas was as much a victim of the war as those of us who were right there in the middle of the bloody conflict. Wars claim their victims in many different ways. They have tentacles that reach beyond the definable violence of battlefields and muddy trenches. They continue to claim casualties long after the physical wounds of shrapnel and gunfire have healed. There is no doubt in my mind that the enforced exile that alienated uncle Nicholas played a crucial part in his illness. As the doctors at the hospital told father the day they discharged him, there was nothing physically wrong with him. Whatever he had was all in his head. He was much too young when he left for London. Too young and too inexperienced to cope with the exhilarating freedoms of his new world; a world that was so different from the one he had left behind.

I was ten when the war started and twenty-one when it ended. In between I lost most of my youth and some of my best friends – Theo, Boyd, Noble, Silas, Killian, Bigboy, and the Nyandoro twins Cain and Abel. These were people I had known since childhood without realising that they harboured grudges far deeper than mine. When they were all killed on the same night trying to cross the Mozambique/Rhodesia border I felt cheated and angry because they had left me out of their doomed plan. And yet I also knew that had they invited me to join I would have found a reason for not going. I was simply not strong enough, or perhaps I was just a coward.

The first time I realised there was a war on was when some of father's people came down from the villages and vowed never to return. Before that I had always thought of the war as something that happened to other people – like freak accidents, natural disasters and fatal diseases.

It so bludgeoned our senses that in the end we became immune to it, like a tired horse that can no longer respond to the stinging pain of the jockey's whip. Each passing day I watched my mother grow old with the violence – embittered, disconsolate and unforgiving. For it was violence that encapsulated in its obscene wholeness the disarray that military confrontation breeds. The nationalist politicians indulged in ritualised displays of reciprocal insults that only served as a tool for the unsympathetic press to explore the dark depths of their ignorance. They waved militant placards and when on television droned on and on like demented sleep-talkers. They proclaimed a fragile unity yet the only thing they had in common, like travellers on the same road, was the destination – not the means of getting there, or the best course to take.

They were an assortment of vainglorious misfits stultified by a communal dearth of intellect. They were men of many promises but few deeds, each pulling in his own direction, each vying to impose his own will. Their speeches were long on emotion and rhetoric but short on ideas. They talked unrealistically of dismantling by proletarian revolution a political system that had been in place for over a century. A political order that was so deeply rooted in the very fabric of the society it had created that it could only be destroyed at considerable expense to the society itself.

The nationalist politicians and the government were like a parasite and its host animal that need each other because of the mutual benefit of an otherwise harmful co-existence. They talked and talked and got nowhere. We listened to both of them, hoping some day they would remove their blinkers and start to make sense. We could see that their promised land would be a tainted utopia, a paradise of emptiness. Yet somehow we listened to them and followed them like columns of compliant somnambulists to the edge of the chasm. Perhaps we were naive to do so, but the situation dictated a response fashioned not by reason but by impulse: the impulse of survival. After the war the same people were to swiftly change sides and stand on rostrums and claim credit for a victory that everybody knew was not theirs.

It is truly amazing how expediency can make people have different memories of the same thing.

When the war intensified, the supplies stopped altogether. A convoy was ambushed near Devil's Hill and fifteen Rhodesian army soldiers killed. So, our side was winning the war, but at what cost? The shops had row upon row of empty shelves as business slackened. There was no bread, sugar, eggs, soap, salt, milk or butter. In fact, there was nothing. Disgruntled regulars took their custom elsewhere. The point was soon reached where the monthly lease repayments on the buildings far exceeded the profits the businesses themselves were making. The three girls father employed, distant cousins brought in as a favour after special pleading from their parents who were worried that continued unemployment might lead them into premature motherhood, were now threatening to take their erstwhile benefactor to court for non-payment of wages. They appreciated their employer's plight but insisted that their own difficulties were now just as pressing.

One afternoon an unmarked van from Zimbabwe Furnishers arrived to cart away our threadbare living-room suite. Mother told prying neighbours that it was going back to be reupholstered. She too had started telling little lies to maintain the family's good name. That night she sat alone be the fire and cried herself to sleep. We sold things in the house so father could pay off his debts. He said his insolvency was a temporary hiccup; a minor occupational blip he would soon overcome. But by then I think even he knew that he was fooling no one. He had to borrow money from one loan shark to pay off another. It became an endless spiral of debt. Sometimes he spent hours in the shops and came back bleary-eyed and pensive. He was a broken man.

I hated the war for what it was doing to him, and what it was making him do to us.

On the day of uncle Nicholas's funeral, father had to go to court again. One of his unpaid creditors had run out of patience and sympathy and issued a writ. The funeral itself was delayed because of heavy seasonal rain. They put the coffin in the living room with its top open and the body garlanded by flowers. There was a heavy, overpowering scent in the air. I went in alone and stared at uncle Nicholas's dead mad face. It was smooth, like a chiselled slab of pasty grey skin. The facial muscles had been frozen into rigid, lopsided snarl that gave his normally pious features the appearance of a petrified gargoyle. His hands were clasped across his chest as if in prayer, the cuffs of his favourite shirt judiciously covering the wrists he had slashed with the bread knife.

His eldest daughter, Michelle, had arrived unannounced from Manchester the previous day for the funeral. She exhausted herself being friendly to the point of sycophancy with everybody she spoke to but it was all in vain. Aunt Emily, uncle Nicholas's widow, had made sure that the girl would feel unwelcome by shamelessly orchestrating a verbal boycott directed at her and her white boyfriend. Most of the people Michelle spoke to spoke back in Shona even though they knew fully well that she was a stranger to both the country and its language. I felt sorry for her, yet at the same time I was also ashamed at allowing myself to be party to such a disgraceful conspiracy. Was Aunt Emily solely responsible for my uncle's fatal madness? It was an unfair charge, but Aunt Emily had always been inclined towards mindless vindictiveness.

Outside the house, women in black veils stood patiently on the deep veranda. Some sang hymns, others chatted about the continuing drought. The men held subdued conversations that centred on the estate of the departed man. By mid-afternoon father had still not appeared on the horizon. My left eye had an autonomous twitch that portended unfavourable news. The rain stopped an hour later and the hearse arrived to lead the procession to the cemetery.

My father had still not returned.

'Bernard... Run to the shop,' said my mother, 'and phone the court to see what has happened to your father. We cannot bury his brother without him here... '

I took the shop keys and dashed off to the smaller of the two grocery shops. There was a telephone in a back office which father used to ring up the Mount Darwin Indian wholesalers who supplied most of his stock. And that was where I found him, slumped across the counter with his wrists cut and his shirtsleeves drenched in brilliant splashes of clotted blood. He was surrounded by unpaid invoices and court summonses. He had been drinking heavily. Several bottles of Bols brandy were on the floor. The Chinese doctor who came from Bindura Hospital said he had been dead for four or five hours at least. There was a bottle of rat poison by his side, long opened but still emitting a faint pungent odour. He had drunk that too. Your father must have really wanted to die, said the doctor, making his astute observation sound as if it was a compliment.

The time of death coincided with the time he had left the house. I knew then that he had never intended to go to the court. That evening I went back to the shop and removed all the court summonses I could find from the office and burnt them in the backyard. I did not think it either fair or necessary for my mother's heartache to be compounded by the revelation that our comfortable lifestyle had been fraudulently financed.

The judge declared him a bankrupt in his absence and ordered sequestration of all movable assets. All the court cases against him were dropped because there was nobody to prosecute. Bailiffs arrived over the next few days to apportion the remaining things in the shops and the house to pay off his creditors. They literally left us in the clothes we were standing in. Mother had to borrow money from relatives to pay for the funeral. Michelle came to tell us that she had booked into a cheaper motel and would be staying for the second funeral. Mother was so touched by this gesture that she dropped her pretended hostility and even invited Michelle and her boyfriend to a meal. But they never came. When I went to their motel I was told they had left urgently. I wrote her a letter, speculatively using one of uncle Nicholas's old addresses, but it came back saying there was not such person known at that address.

We moved house after that but we could not erase the memory of father's death. One cannot rid a room of its bad associations by rearranging the furniture. Father died in April 1981, exactly a year after Independence. Those debts accumulated during the war proved too much even for a man of his resilience. Like uncle Nicholas and so many others, he survived the war only to die of its effects when the peace arrived.

5

The Time of Locusts

Even God is deprived of this one thing only:
the power to undo what has been done.

(Agathon, in *Aristotle, Nichomachean Ethics*)

Portia was born on a cold day in July 1957 at the mission hospital
in the Mapfukunde valley. Her mother, Hajiko, who had a heart
condition, died shortly after the birth. As Leonard Nzou cradled
his newborn daughter in his arms he shed tears of joy and prayed
that the child would not grow to be fat and ugly, and that when she
was of age she would find herself a kind and considerate husband.
The last thing he needed was the burden of a miserable old spinster
spending all her earthly days with him at the same house where she
had grown up, as had been the case with one of his paternal aunts.
The aunt eventually died in the same house she had been born in
and lived in all her adult life – unloved, alone and angry at the way
life had treated her.

Nzou's prayers were duly answered. Portia grew up to be a
beautiful woman, though not quite as beautiful as her mother, and
married a young fisherman from a family well respected in the
village. Portia's husband, Hubert Chiware, was an industrious young
man, spending long hours in his narrow boat trawling for bream
and whitebait in the nearby Wiltshire River. Hubert always caught

more fish than he needed for his family. He would generously give some of his catch to his in-laws and the family of his elder brother, Rujeko, who had been injured in an industrial accident. Because of a permanently damaged leg, Rujeko now required the use of a crutch to get by. The disability compensation promised by the company, where he had sustained his injury, was taking a long time to come through.

In February 1977, Hubert and Portia were looking forward to the birth of their first child. Then the war arrived in the village. Within weeks, a peaceful, pastoral community was transferred into a fully militarised war zone. Government soldiers moved around in menacing convoys, sometimes mounting roadblocks where they demanded to see people's identification particulars and, if they were strangers, asking them what their business was in the village. Those who failed to produce the papers were arrested and taken away and sometimes never seen again. Rather than be conscripted into the government army, a lot of the young men chose to leave their villages and join the same forces the government wanted them to fight.

For Hubert it was a painful decision, leaving his young beautiful wife and their unborn baby. But he had no choice. The decision to join the war on the anti-government side had been made for him by others. By the beginning of 1975 young men in the village were absconding daily across the border to join the guerrillas. In April 1977 Hubert packed a bag and disappeared into the bush under cover of darkness. It was the same year an invasion of locusts from the east caused great hunger by destroying the maize crop. Fearful of being betrayed to the authorities, Hubert had not disclosed his plans to anybody, not even to his wife. The man who recruited him had told him not to give his relatives any information.

'People who are tortured will always talk. Better they don't even know anything.'

It took Portia months to get over her husband's departure. Abandoned at the age of eighteen and in only her second year of marriage, she did not know what to do. With no means of supporting herself she had been left exposed, like a fish stranded on the bed of a dried river. She would sit alone in her hut for long periods, confused and contemplative, silent and unmoving. She would only be jolted out of these frequent reveries by the local children coming from school as they made their way along the narrow path at the back of her hut, shouting on top of their voices the nonsensical rhymes they would have learnt at the mission school that day:

'*Old McDonald had a farm, eeyah-eeyah-oh..*'

Hubert's elder brother Rujeko, as the titular head of the family, took it upon himself to ensure his sister-in-law wanted for nothing. During the first few months after his brother's departure, Rujeko, whose compensation money had eventually come through, provided Portia with all she needed for her daily sustenance. Sometimes he would give her money to buy herself a dress or a pair of shoes. When Portia's baby arrived, he would give her money to buy napkins and baby food. To Portia he was everything a caring brother-in-law should be. But then, after about a year, his attitude changed. He began telling Portia that a beautiful woman like her should not live by herself. He also told her that it was the tradition in the village that if a man died his brother had a duty to marry his widow.

'Our ancestors have always followed this custom because it means a widow will continue to live the life she was accustomed to.'

'But my husband is not dead, *baba mukuru*,' Portia would say whenever the suggestion of marrying her brother-in-law was put to her.

'You cannot wait forever, *amainini*. Maybe Hubert will not come back. Who knows what happened wherever he went? Marry me, and I will look after you and your son.'

'I cannot do that, *baba mukuru*. My husband is not dead. I can feel it in my bones. I will wait as long as is necessary.'

After all else failed he tried to win her affections through self-pity.

'Do you shun me because I am a cripple, *amainini*?'

'I cannot marry you. What if Hubert then turns up the very next day? You and I will have committed adultery.'

Rujeko let the subject rest, but not before he had warned his sister-in-law that she would live to regret her decision.

'Life is as brief as a dream, *amainini*. By the time you realise what you have lost, you might no longer be in a position to retrieve it.'

In 1979 the war ended. Not in the bushes and valleys where it had been fought with such unimaginable and unrelenting brutality, but in a room in West London where the delegates to an all-party conference finally agreed to bury the hatchet and share the peace pipe. The war had lasted either sixteen or eighty-three years. It all depends on what one takes as the starting point – the 1896 uprisings against the colonial settlers or the 1966 Battle of Sinoia. But end it did, and after the ceasefire there was much jubilation as families long separated by curfews and divided loyalties were reunited. But others perished in the trenches of sacrifice and did not return. Hubert Chiware, Portia Nzou's husband, the intrepid fisherman of the Mapfukunde valley, was one of those who did not return.

The son born in his absence was nearly three when Independence came, a robust and hyperactive toddler whose early years were only blighted by a mild attack of German measles. Portia waited for months to show the boy his father for the first time, but it was all in vain. Hubert did not return. In the four years of her husband's absence, Portia had grown cynical and hard-hearted with her disconsolation. Somehow, she knew she had to force herself to look forward to the future, even though her uneventful life had long become trapped in the ruins of the past. She had stopped living, because she could not start a new life without completely severing the threads that linked her to the old one.

In the first few days after his departure she had cried every night until her eyes had no more tears. The pain of loneliness was like a jagged piece of flint chipping away at her heart. On some nights she had dreams in which he came back, stood by her bed, his fisherman's basket brimming with fish, their eyes glassy and their silver scales dulled by the pale moonlight. Sometimes he would be standing so close she could feel his hot breath fanning her face. And then something would happen – a dog outside barking, a goat in the pen bleating unexpectedly – and the dream would be gone. And then once more she would be alone in the hut, alone with the humid night and its sullen layers of silence.

Each day she sat outside her hut and stared at the green grass of the rolling hills beyond the valley, wondering where he was, what he was doing. Was he dead? Was he alive? Where was his last resting place? The wind that jolted her front door at night would wake her up in a feverish sweat. Confused with sleep, she would think maybe Hubert had come back, or had sent an emissary with a message to assure her that he was alive and well. But he never came back, and as the days became months, and the months became years, all she consoled herself with was the spitting image of himself he had left behind – their son. She saw Hubert's face every time she looked at him, and she heard his voice every time the boy spoke or cried out.

Four more years went by. Nothing was heard of Hubert Chiware. He was assumed dead; life had to go on for those he had left behind. After another three years a memorial service was held in his home village to enable his spirit to finally rest in peace. As is the tradition, his earthly belongings were shared between his relatives. His son, also named Hubert, was given his father's long fishing boat. He was not quite ten, but had already shown a prowess for handling fishing nets that indicated he would be as good a fisherman as his father. As was also the custom, Rujeko, Hubert's elder brother, took Portia as his second wife. She finally relented only because time had healed her emotional wounds. Rujeko already had a wife and three sons. Now in a wheelchair, he declared to his new in-laws and his relatives that he would look after his new family just as if it was his own. He owed it to his late brother Hubert, whose life had been sacrificed for a noble cause.

Within two years Portia had given birth to a bouncy baby girl.

A year later, she gave birth to a son. Rujeko, overjoyed that his ancestors had blessed him with an heir, arranged a great feast in the village to celebrate the occasion. He sent out word inviting all the villagers to come and share in his joy. Several beasts were slaughtered and the merry-making lasted until the early hours. The chief of the village came to the festivities and made a speech about how important it was to maintain traditional values, as Rujeko had done by marrying his late brother's wife. Leonard Nzou also showered praise on his new son-in-law, saying that he was lucky to have, not one, but two sons-in-law from the Chiware family.

The following day was a Sunday. As was usual, Rujeko's two wives took their children to church, leaving him lying in the bedroom recovering from the previous day's excesses. Portia was the first one to come back from church. She always left earlier than the others so she could start preparations for Sunday lunch. She arrived home and found the front door of the hut she shared with Rujeko ajar. Since Rujeko now had two wives, he needed two huts for his wives and spent alternate nights with each one. After his son's party the previous day he had spent the night with Portia.

Inside the hut there was no sign of Rujeko. Portia knew that her husband never ventured far from the huts in his wheelchair. She went back outside and walked around the perimeter of their home, hoping he was somewhere nearby. Then she met a local herdboy who told her that he had seen Rujeko talking to a tall man he didn't recognise.

'Where were they?'

'By the big *munhondo* tree, near your goat pen.'

Portia went to the goat pen, but there was no sign of Rujeko or the man he had been seen talking to. Portia wondered who the mysterious stranger was. The ground was wet and soft, and from the goat pen she could see the track marks made by the wheelchair. She followed the tracks for about a quarter of a mile into the valley towards the Wiltshire River, wondering how Rujeko had managed to get the strength to push the wheelchair such a distance – unless, of course, the mysterious man had helped him. But there were no footprints to suggest that anybody had walked alongside the wheelchair.

When she got to the edge of the river the tracks disappeared suddenly. She stood on the river's edge, her heart filling with dread. No, she whispered to herself, he couldn't have. How could he? Panic-stricken, she started to run back to the village, screaming wildly. Near the goat pen she met her father-in-law and some of his male relatives. They stopped her and asked her to calm down. She told them she was looking for her husband, Rujeko.

'I don't know where he is. I have just come from the river. He went there in his wheelchair; maybe he fell into the water. We have to go back there.'

I have some news for you Portia,' said her father-in-law.

'Something has happened to Rujeko?'

'We don't really know yet. But this morning, when you were in church, Hubert Chiware came back.'

The shock of the news jolted her so much she fell to her knees.

'Hubert? He's alive?'

'Yes. He's alive.'

'The war ended many years ago, but he did not come back. Now he comes back?'

'He said he didn't know the war was over. He has been living in a cave in the mountains all these years.'

'What do I do now? It's been such a long time.'

'Yes, it has.'

'You spoke to him… What did he say?'

'He says he wants his wife and son.'

Portia said nothing. She just shook her head, muttering incoherently to herself.

'And Rujeko? Does he know his brother is back?'

'Hubert went to see him this morning when you were at church. They talked.'

'What did they talk about?'

'Hubert would not say.'

'Maybe Hubert knows where Rujeko went?'

Her father-in-law said nothing.

'Where is Hubert now?'

'Hubert is at my house. He is waiting for us to go back and settle this matter. He wants to know why we married you off to his brother.'

'Nearly ten years I waited for him. I loved him and then he abandoned me. Rujeko is my husband now. If anything is going to be discussed, Rujeko has to be there.'

'Nobody knows where Rujeko is, Portia. After Hubert visited him this morning he went to the river and a herdboy swears that he saw him throwing himself into the water. Some of the village men are dredging the river, trying to recover his body.'

'Kill himself? But, why?'

'He told Hubert that he could not live with the shame he felt. After that Hubert left him and came to my house.'

Portia sat down on the dry grass and began sobbing softly. The men looked at her and said nothing. They understood and respected her grief; there was nothing they could say to her. Ahead, in the haze of the midday sun, some children were coming from the Sunday school, shouting at the top of their voices the new hymn they had learnt that day:

'What a friend we have in Jesus...'

By mid-afternoon the news of Rujeko's death had already spread. Portia, still in a state of shock, sat in her hut surrounded by her relatives. Rujeko's first wife sat in her hut surrounded by her relatives. Although married to the same man, there was no love lost between the two grieving widows. In the distance could be heard the sound of mourning as women from adjacent homesteads walked towards Rujeko Chiware's home for the funeral wake.

Rujeko's body was never found. There were man-eating crocodiles in the Wiltshire River. It was assumed that one of these monsters dragged his body off to its lair; or maybe the strong currents took it downstream to wherever the river finally exhausted itself. During his brother's funeral Hubert Chiware saw his son for the first time, and the boy showed his father the long fishing boat that had once been his and told him how good he was at trawling bream and whitebait. After an appropriate passage of time, as was the traditional custom in the village, Hubert Chiware married his late brother Rujeko's wife Portia.

6

A Secret Sin

Time is longer than rope, Jerry.
Nothing lasts forever, except sin.

Thirty years lost in the diaspora. That was you, Jerry Machingauta. Your father was on his deathbed when you came back from England, a frail old man dying from an unknown illness that was slowly eating him from the inside. He had sores in his mouth and the power of sight had long gone from his eyes.

That first day you visited him in hospital he felt the skin of your face with the tips of quivering fingers and then asked you to sit on the edge of the bed next to him so he could feel the warmth of your body, the smell of your sweat. You and he had always been the same blood, the same flesh. Your lives had been tethered to a collective fate, your destinies conjoined.

In your tender years it was your father who encouraged you to pursue your studies, assured you that some day perseverance would engender its own reward. You were the only one amongst his three children who showed any promise, the only one who seemed destined for greater things. You dreamt of pursuing a career in medicine or engineering and your father's unwavering support enabled you to have a clear vista of your fate. And when you finally left for England your father warned you about the dangers of unknown cities, about the bright lights of Babylon camouflaging a deep internal rot.

In those early London days, you heeded his warning. You were constantly on your guard because in the war-torn townships you had left behind you had seen too many lives succumb to temptation. The roll-call of tragedy was inexhaustible, the departure of a relative or a dear friend always a catastrophic and incalculable loss. You went to the all-night funeral wakes, the late afternoon burials. You would dutifully stand, sometimes in the pouring rain, staring at the mounds of fresh earth marking the new graves and listening to the eulogies.

'Man that is born of woman has but a few days to live.'

Your mother died when you were young and the people who were closest to you from her side of the family were her three sisters – Esther Mushonga, Veronica Sendera and Sarah Mushita – maternal surrogates who gave you more love than you could ever handle in a single lifetime. At your mother's funeral it was these same people who wept the loudest, prompting your grandmother to sigh and shake her grey-haired head:

'If such furious lamentations cannot wake poor Hilda from the sleep of God then nothing else will.'

But your father was the one who was always there to guide you through those early difficult years, the beacon that shone bright at the end of your troubled journey through childhood; the one person who encouraged you to get through those difficult exams at the end of each term. Do whatever you want to do well or don't do it at all, he would tell you. Because an eel caught by the tail is only half-caught.

Those exams.

The desks lined up in rooms which seemed vast, smelling of the collective fear of an ill-prepared army aware of its fatal limitations, the soft rustle of crisp paper, the affected coughs of the candidates that betrayed something more than just nervousness.

'You may begin.'

Question papers fearfully torn out of their polythene covers and then the contents briefly scrutinised amidst silent howls of derision and relief. The ominous ticking of the clock on the wall, its two hands always split into a configuration resembling a mocking grin, the intrusive pandemonium of peripheral activities – of pencils and pens being readied for unknown battles, of desks and chairs being pointlessly repositioned, of handbags and coats clattering to the floor, and then the invigilator's voice booming like that of a drill sergeant:

'You have exactly five minutes.'

There was nobody waiting for you at the airport when you arrived because nobody knew you were coming. There was none of the incandescent jubilation that accompanied your departure; none of the wild ululating and cheering that followed your over-confident swagger towards the plane that balmy day in October 1974.

After completing the arrivals formalities, you sat alone in the back of a battered taxi, your route to the city centre taking you past the absurdly fortified houses of the southern suburbs and the hard-labour prisoners working on the verges of the road, pale and hunched in the morning mist like winter ghosts.

The telegram sent by one of your paternal aunts the previous week contained two terse lines that conveyed a grim message:

'Your father is very sick. You have to be here.'

How different it had been that day when you left, a starry-eyed nineteen-year-old with a grand vision of a bright future. It was the first time you had ever been on a plane, and it both excited and frightened you; when you looked outside the plane seemed to be floating on a mound of static fluffiness.

All round you clouds were suspended in mid-air like body parts floating in jars of preservative. And where the clouds were parted by the plane's heaving fuselage they hung in the sky like fat bubbles and the ground below seemed to spread forever in all directions, a disfigured and patchy mosaic with roads and streams spread out like arteries.

'Tell me about England, my son. Tell me about the land of the white man. The land of the BBC, The Queen, cricket and snow.'

And so you sat on the edge of the bed and told your dying father about those things, details he wanted to hear, an affirmation of lifetime myths that had adhered for so long they could now no longer be discarded. To delete the old man's perception of 'Overseas' would have been an unnecessary cruelty. You told him about the red double-decker buses as huge as suburban houses and the underground trains that moved with the stealth of serpents in the dark belly of the earth.

You told him about the tall glass buildings of the West End and the historic steel and concrete bridges of the River Thames that united opposite shores without touching the water, structures that ingeniously spanned space without ever seeming to belong to it.

You told him about the shopping malls of Wood Green and Croydon that were so vast and complex it took hours to explore all the shops, and about the same amount of time to locate one's car in the car park afterwards. You told him about shoppers scurrying up and down Oxford Street and Tottenham Court Road in numbers so great it was like watching the wildebeest and antelope migrations of the Mapfukunde valley.

'And your life in England? How was your life in England, my son?'

But certain things are better left unsaid, Jerry. Some revelations serve no useful purpose. Talk is cheap, word gets round. You couldn't tell your father about your secret life in the land of the BBC, The Queen, cricket and snow. You couldn't tell him about the numerous white girls you had gone out with, a secret sin that hung around your neck like a monumental yoke of shame now that you were back amongst your own people. You couldn't tell him about Zoey, Virna, Macy, Vaneshree and Mitzi.

First there was Zoey Bellingham, a bespectacled and loose-limbed teenager whom you met in a pub in 1977 and lived with for a whole year without her parents' consent. Her face wore a permanent wide-mouthed and goggle-eyed expression of mild surprise – like someone who had recently been revived by artificial respiration.

She was always bumping into things, Zoey, as if her blinkered eyes were firmly glued to the sides of her head and she viewed the world around her through a monochromatic wide-angled aperture of confusion.

You couldn't tell your father that after Zoey there was Virna Fioravanti from Sicily, she of hair the colour of burnt sienna and the beguiling Mona Lisa smile. What you liked about Virna was that she didn't have any of Zoey's assorted psychotic manias. You liked her amoebic and phantom-like unobtrusiveness, her uncanny ability to become inconspicuous by imperceptibly diluting her presence.

Whenever some of your friends came over to discuss the worsening political situation in your country, Virna would be there, but not really there – like a chameleon that can adopt the colours of its background at will and disintegrate into a blur of anonymity.

On the other hand, she was into Chuck Berry and Little Richard and Howlin' Wolf, the raucous good-time music of Memphis and the Mississippi Delta, and the walls of her bedroom were adorned with shiny portraits of her idols in tight suits and pointed shoes. Every night she dragged you to a rowdy pub on the high street where an old Negro blues guitarist sang slow painful songs about slavery and emancipation and other associated ills of the black man's burden.

No, you couldn't tell your father about Mitzi.

You remember Mitzi?

Mitzi Rosenberg of the hoarse laugh and cherub cheeks. She was your second white girlfriend and you were her second black boyfriend. Her first African boyfriend was a bad-tempered Nigerian who beat her black and blue and left her after seven months with three broken teeth and a mind befuddled with bad memories.

It was a gloomy Thursday during the arctic winter of 1979 when you met Mitzi. The Liberal Party had funded a symposium on African Nationalism at the School of Oriental and African Studies. You went because some friends invited you. Mitzi went because her friend was one of the speakers.

You had met Mitzi briefly a few weeks before that, when you took part in some hospital's fund-raising marathon together and afterwards she joined you and your posse of home-boys on a riotous pub-crawl that took in its stride seven pubs and three wine bars across five boroughs. That night you and three of your mates ended up freezing to the bone in the cells of a South London police station for being 'drunk and disorderly'.

After the SOAS symposium there was a wine bar in the foyer. You mingled with politicians and academic celebrities. People you had only seen on television and in the newspapers. You spent fifteen minutes chatting to a plump breathless woman who did the weather forecast on one of the television channels. She had yellow teeth and terrible halitosis. She reminded you of Miss Penelope Leggett, your English teacher at St Phillip's secondary school.

The weather woman's name was Bridget and she told you in her spare time she wrote an agony column for a teenage magazine and kept a three-foot South American iguana in her bedroom. Your major disappointment was that in the flesh she seemed shorter than she did on television. When she put her hand on your thigh and asked you what you were doing later on in the evening you made your excuses and left discreetly.

Emboldened by the joint you had shared with a West Indian student in the car park you walked across to where Mitzi was and ensnared her with your Neanderthal charm. Shy at first, she told you she was an Archaeology student and had just spent the last two months of her gap year working with forty other students on an Inca dig in the central highlands of Peru.

She told you of her amazing travels on three continents during her year out. She told you of the rock cliff tombs of southern China, the ceremonial dancing grounds of ancient Polynesia, the fossilised bodies unearthed from ancient peat bogs in Europe. Lindow Man, Grauballe Man, Tollund Man. You told her you were studying Civil Engineering at Imperial College, that one day you would design a bridge to heaven to convey the souls of the newly dead. She laughed and said you were quite crazy.

That weekend you went to the Leicester Square Odeon and sat through two and half hours of 'Apocalypse Now'. Because you didn't really like war epics you lost the plot halfway through the film and spent the rest of the time giving Mitzi a feel under her crinkly poloneck. Your kind of film was the one with the misunderstood tragic hero who barely makes it through the final reel. James Cagney in 'Angels with Dirty Faces', Jack Lemmon in 'The China Syndrome', for example.

Apart from the twice weekly doses of frenzied sex in her dingy bed-sit above a spice shop on the Fulham Road the two of you soon discovered you had very little in common. She was into female emancipation and nuclear disarmament and existentialist philosophy. CND, Germaine Greer, Søren Kirkegaard. You had little time for her exotic highbrow pursuits. The truth is, such things had never been central to your existence. You grew up in a dusty colonial outpost on a diet of cheap westerns, gaudy photo-action comics and two-reel 'B' movies. She couldn't understand your interest in John Wayne and Roy Rogers.

You always felt embarrassed to tell her about your past, your illiterate parents and your half-crazed brother Chamu who joined the army on a whim and came back with a calcified stump where his left leg had been. You didn't tell Mitzi about your younger sister Estelle who emerged from her rebellious teenage years burdened with the responsibility of bringing up three children from three different fathers. You didn't tell her about the ignominious shame your father felt at having to live with the eternal disgrace of Estelle's totem-less offspring. You never mentioned your aunt Peregrina Masuku who spent fifteen years in America and came back in 1973 with a Texan drawl and the clothes on her back.

One night, Mitzi told you about her family, migrant Polish Jews who had escaped the grinding poverty and hunger of their native country in the 1930s and settled in Central Europe. Half her father's family had perished in the gas ovens of Auschwitz. That day she opened a dog-eared picture album and pulled out a photograph of her great-aunt Tanya Rosenberg. The picture had been taken by one of the Soviet soldiers who had liberated the camp.

'There. That's my aunt Tanya,' she said, pointing to a forlorn scarecrow standing amidst a mound of bug-eyed skeletons.

'I don't hate Hitler for what he did,' she said, 'It wasn't his fault.'

You didn't tell Mitzi that when you were ten you started creating your own personalised nightmares, that you would visit your uncle Ephraim at the African hospital where he worked as a clerk and watch through a back window the daily ritual of white-coated mortuary attendants silently wheeling bloated cadavers to the post-mortem labs. That afterwards you would retch your guts out and go for days without eating or drinking until you became dizzy with hunger and dehydration.

You didn't tell her that when you were thirteen you wrote a story about a one-eyed giant who lived in the massive sewage ponds on the edge of the township and came out at night to prey on newborn babies. Miss Penelope Leggett gave you two out of ten and wrote 'See Me' at the bottom of your composition. You never did, because that was the week you spent at home bedridden with a convenient attack of mumps.

You didn't tell Mitzi that at fourteen you told your parents about the fire-eating demons that visited you at night and made you sleepwalk in ever-increasing circles until you fell down with exhaustion. You didn't tell her that on hot summer nights you had bad dreams that gave you nosebleeds and made you wet your bed, that you had a mortal dread of cockroaches and black ants, or that in your early teenage years you drew gory pictures that scared your siblings and so worried your parents they sought the help of your school's headmaster. He told them there was nothing to worry about; that it was just a pubescent phase that would soon pass.

You didn't tell Mitzi that as you grew older you couldn't tell the dreams from reality, that as the voices in your head grew louder the only way you could fight them was by staying awake all night. You became a creature of darkness, walking the township streets at night like a stray dog because you could not fight that which you could not see, could not touch, could not understand.

Your first suicide attempt was when you were eighteen, shortly before you went to England. You told your father it was the only way you could fight the demons. Fortunately for you, the malaria tablets nauseated you so much you vomited them. Your father called a priest who prayed for you and said the good Lord always watches over his flock.

You couldn't tell your father that after Mitzi left you because of your alcoholism you abandoned your studies and became a regular at the pubs in your neighbourhood frequented by self-made failures like yourself. The demons of your childhood had returned to haunt you. You quickly became the star attraction at the high street bars, daily showing off the little knowledge garnered in your nine months at university to anybody who bothered to listen. To make ends meet you got as job as a night-shift packer in a supermarket, but they made you redundant after four months. They told you there was an economic recession; last one in first one out.

Now officially an illegal immigrant, you went to live in a grimy northern town where the authorities couldn't track you down. And that's where you have been living for the past ten years, with a West Indian woman ten years older than you who took you in because she felt sorry for you. She let you share her bed and gave you a decent meal every day. When you left you told her you were coming back but deep down inside you knew you were not going to do so.

'Always tell the truth, my son. The good thing about telling the truth is you don't have to remember what you said.'

That was what your father always told you during your formative years. The truth passes through fire and does not burn. But certain things are better left unsaid, Jerry. Some revelations serve no useful purpose.

You couldn't tell your dying father that England was not the paradise of your teenage dreams. You couldn't tell him how you hated London, the bleak grey weather and the nauseating pollution; the aloofness of the city's disparate clans and the affected camaraderie of the shaggily dressed bohemian oddballs who frequented the students' union bar at your college.

And you couldn't tell him that in the thirty years that was your secret life in the land of the BBC, The Queen, cricket and snow you had achieved nothing. That like your aunt Peregrina Masuku you had wasted thirty years of your life and come back to your father's deathbed with only the clothes on your back and a baggage of bittersweet memories.

Time is longer than rope, Jerry.

7

Blunt Force Trauma

There is no fear where there is faith.
(Native American proverb)

Sometimes small actions lead to major reactions.

One chilly afternoon in June 2008, in the small dark space in front
of the loading bay at Parirenyatwa Hospital mortuary, I had to
positively identify the body of my cousin, Eldridge Gunguwo,
before the workers from the funeral home took it away for the pre-
burial preparations. His face was serene and peaceful, as if he was
sleeping and would soon be up and going about his usual business.
Since Eldridge had died under mysterious circumstances a forensic
post-mortem was mandatory because the police suspected foul play.
His body had been found two days after he was last seen, dumped
in a piece of waste ground about three kilometres from the house
he shared with his wife Melody and two young daughters, Maxine
and Roxanne.

Electricity had become a luxury for most people, and Eldridge,
a qualified electrician, made a decent living carrying out solar
installations and repairing generators. The job often took him to
far-flung parts of the country. Sometimes he would be away from
his family for several days at a time. But whenever work required

him to travel he told Melody where he was going and for how long. This time she had been mystified when he did not return from work at his usual time and her calls to his cellular phone went unanswered until she gave up trying. That was around midnight. When she had not heard from him by nightfall the next day, she called me over and we went and made a report to the police. The police told us that a grown-up adult with a wife and two children could not just disappear into thin air. They assured Melody that sooner or later he would turn up.

'A person does not officially become missing until after forty-eight hours. But married men can do all sorts of funny things,' said one of the police officers, without elaborating. The comment was probably meant to reassure Melody but it only increased her anxiety.

'If we have any news we will be in touch,' said the policeman.

We drove back to the house and waited for news.

The last person to see Eldridge alive, apart from those who had been responsible for his death, was his friend and business partner, Simon Pfende. He told mourners gathered at Eldridge's house that on the fateful Friday afternoon his colleague had told him that he was going to finish work early because he wanted to attend a meeting at an office building in the city centre.

'We don't know when or how he died,' said Simon. 'And the police have said we can't bury him until a forensic post-mortem is carried out.'

Eldridge was my friend and closest confidant from our kindergarten days. He was actually a sort of cousin – our mothers were distant relatives – but a lot of people didn't know that. When we were growing up we all wanted to be like Eldridge's older brother, Hector, who loomed large in our early lives – big and colourful like a comic book hero. One day, when he was about eighteen years old, Hector had a dream that changed his life, like Saul on the road to Damascus. The next day he wagered his entire pay as a panel-beater's assistant on a hundred-to-one outsider in the July Handicap – a four-year old filly called 'Yellow Peril' – and won a small fortune. The following year Hector went to America and has not been heard of since.

At school, Eldridge was a sickly toddler plagued by a multitude of respiratory problems. He would cough until his face was blue. He always yearned for attention, always wanted to be at the centre of things. When people ignored him, he would become moody and unpredictable, playing the part of the introspective, troubled hero to perfection. When we started Grade One we sat next to each other in the back row where we could safely carry out small acts of mischief away from the teacher's censorious eye. We got away with murder because our first-grade teacher was Mr Wesley Munyoro, an elderly and gentle soul who was as blind as a bat and couldn't see further than the tip of his crooked nose. We called him 'Rip van Winkle' because most of the time he gave us work to do and then promptly fell asleep in his chair.

In those early years, Eldridge suffered from a minor speech impediment and as a result he was shy and withdrawn. He would eventually overcome this particular handicap, just as he would overcome other minor hurdles that confronted him in the early years of his life. But he would always be the odd man out, Eldridge, the square peg that could never fit into a round hole. And yet he was curious to the point of annoyance. Nature mystified him; he could never understand why there were earthquakes, volcanic eruptions, floods and storms – or how something as breathtakingly beautiful as a butterfly began life as a maggot.

I was always amused by his dedication to such trivia but he would always say if one understood why things were the way were, it was easy to understand why life was the way it was. Perhaps he had a point, but whatever it was, it was lost on me. I remember when we were in Grade Seven we accompanied his mother to see his father who had been committed to the psychiatric unit at Harare Hospital. Solomon Gunguwo was a mean-tempered and malevolent individual who didn't get on with most people. He had been taken to the hospital after attacking a senior workmate with an axe handle, accusing the man of sending goblins to bewitch him and using *mbashto* to stop him from being promoted.

The psychiatric unit was a strange and surreal annexe at the back of the main hospital, a dilapidated single-story building submerged in tall grass and surrounded by ponds of raw sewage. The wards smelt of disinfectant and stale urine and I remember being struck by the whiteness of everything around us – the whiteness of the fluorescent lights, the whiteness of the walls and the ceilings, the whiteness of the nurses' uniforms, the whiteness of the inmates' teeth. Even the drinking water, a frothy deluge that spewed out of the rusty copper taps like a tsunami, was milky white. When Eldridge's father came out of the psychiatric unit he soon became a hopeless alcoholic. Early in 1977 he went to live in his home village three hundred kilometres away, sustained by a generous Rhodesia Railways pension and a slew of rural concubines. Eldridge and his mother had endured enough of the man's violent mood swings and chose to remain in the township.

The one thing I admired about Eldridge was his sheer dogged determination, his desire to succeed whatever the size of the odds stacked against him. He was a good sportsman but not so good academically. He could do the hundred-metre sprint in eleven seconds flat. I remember once he won a prize for Art but still finished second from last in his class that term. He felt elated and disappointed at the same time, like a soccer player who gets the man-of-the-match award when his team has lost the game.

We wrote our O-Levels in the same year and I managed to pass seven out of the eight I had written. Eldridge passed four, and such was his determination to attain the magical figure of five O-Levels he spent the next two years studying hard until he passed that elusive fifth subject. After finishing our O-Levels we did a basic electrical course at the polytechnic but neither of us could secure any gainful employment.

We did what most unemployed people of our age did: we drank a lot of beer, smoked a lot of weed and chased a lot of girls. By then Eldridge had become a real ladies' man, knowing just the right things to say and do in the company of the finer sex. We spent most of our days at Auntie Beulah Chikoko's unlicensed bottle store in

Warren Park 'D', nursing lukewarm Lion lagers and dissecting the latest political gossip. Auntie Bee, a large bulbous woman with a loose tongue and even looser morals, was not really our aunt but we called her that because she went to the same church as our parents and both of us had known her since we were infants.

Warm beer was not the only known hazard at auntie Bee's illegal establishment. One also had to contend with the constant advances of an elderly pair of resident prostitutes and the ever-present danger of a midnight police raid. Auntie Bee had been pretty enough in her early years to have won the 'Miss African Queen' pageant twice, but in the ensuing years her fine attributes were mercilessly ravaged by a lifestyle whose main features were a bad diet and carnal over-indulgence.

Although she often claimed to have walked down the matrimonial aisle seven times, auntie Bee could only remember her life with three of her husbands, details of the rest seeming to have long disappeared down a black hole of the alcohol-induced amnesia that beset her in her mid-forties. Auntie Bee's real age was a closely guarded secret, and a sure way to incur her legendary wrath was to enquire about her age during the lavish birthday parties she threw for herself to commemorate each successfully lived year.

In 1992, when Eldridge was barely twenty-two, he moved to Johannesburg and for two years worked on the hazardous streets of Hillbrow. He had been to South Africa the previous year to take part in the Comrades Marathon and had fallen in love with the country. He first worked as a vendor of soapstone curios and other artefacts from his home country, and then after securing a counterfeit work permit, as an auto-electrician for a minicab company operating mainly in the meandering streets of Berea, Yeoville and Braamfontein. A friend who worked for a finance house arranged an inexpensive loan and Eldridge managed to convince his employer to sell him the mini-cab business. Within eight months he had a fleet of five vehicles and employed four full-time drivers.

At his invitation, I visited him in December 1991 and he picked me up from Park Station in a charcoal black Honda Accord. I could see he was proud of the car by the way he cradled the steering wheel and the furtive glance he cast in my direction when I heard the engine roar into life for the first time. On the way to his small rented apartment in Marshalltown he told me that Johannesburg was a place of endless pleasures and opportunities, a true paradise on earth. I could not help feeling envious of his success because in the township where we had both grown up, Jo'burg was every unemployed youth's dream destination, London and New York included.

'If you can't make money in this town, you will never make money anywhere else,' Eldridge said as the car cruised down a wide and dipping avenue, shouting to be heard above the deafening din of the car radio.

That evening Eldridge took me on a whistle-stop tour of his favourite haunts in Hillbrow. There was an ephemeral *ad hoc* quality about the place – as if the buildings had come first and then the roads and alleyways had been haphazardly threaded through the leftover space. He took me to a crowded club and then to a striptease bar where thin pasty-faced Asian women gyrated around chrome-plated poles. Then afterwards we had a quick supper in a busy fast-food restaurant near Joubert Park.

Later on, as we drove back to his place, Eldridge told me Johannesburg had its hidden dangers, like the gangs who followed travellers from the coach station and airport and robbed them of their belongings when they arrived at their destinations. He said it was easy to get guns in Jo'burg, and just as easy to become a victim of the same firearms. Life in Johannesburg, he said sighing, was a daily struggle against becoming a crime statistic.

But in the middle of 2004, after Eldridge had lived in South Africa for almost a decade and a half, somebody broke into the premises on Commissioner Street that housed his minicab business and set everything on fire. The unknown arsonists also torched Eldridge's entire fleet of nine cars and three minibuses parked outside. A driver sleeping in one of the parked cars was badly beaten up and left for dead. The following day one of Eldridge's South African friends advised him to leave the country.

'They hate your success because you are a *kwerekwere*,' said the man, using the derogatory term the locals reserved for fellow Africans from beyond their borders.

'They don't like successful foreigners here. The next thing is that they will come after you.'

And that was how Eldridge's sojourn in the land of his dreams came to an abrupt end. A few months after his return he met and fell in love with Melody Nyamweda, a young teacher at a primary school in Warren Park 'D'. Their daughter Maxine was born at the beginning of 2005; Roxanne followed at the beginning of 2006.

Because I do not own a car, Simon Pfende offered to drive me to the hospital where the post-mortem was to be carried out. The police at Avondale Police Station had told me that relatives of the deceased were required to be at the hospital in case the pathologist wished to ask questions relating to the circumstances of death. The man arrived around ten in the morning, accompanied by two smart-suited detectives from the CID Homicide division. Whenever foul play was suspected it was mandatory for the investigators of that particular case to be present during the post-mortem. The relatives of the deceased sat in two rows of wooden desks facing the entrance of the small office. There was an air of bored resignation in the room, as hospital staff worked at their own leisurely pace.

The doctor was a short hyperactive woman with stringy black hair and owlish spectacles that looked as if they had been made for someone with a much broader face. We would later learn from the assistant inspector at the police post that she was a foreigner and that her grasp of English was rudimentary. She sat at a corner desk in the assistant inspector's office and meticulously scrutinised the files that had been put aside for her. She would constantly adjust her oversized spectacles with a deft movement of the bridge of her nose. She glanced at the two detectives who had accompanied her and shook her head. Then she addressed the assistant inspector in charge of the police post.

'Four PM's, but only two police... Where is police? Where is police? No police, no PM. You know is strict government regulation for police to be there...'

'Police coming, Dr Hernandez,' said the assistant inspector, imitating the doctor's singsong English.

'Hernandez is from Cuba. She speaks only Spanish,' said the assistant inspector as if in response to our bland stares.

'So how does she write the post-mortem reports?' asked a huge white-haired man sitting next to me. I had earlier held a brief conversation with him during which he informed me had had come in connection with the death of his eleven-month old granddaughter found dead in a case of suspected infanticide. The baby had been force-fed a mysterious substance by its mother, who had subsequently been arrested and was currently languishing at the remand prison awaiting a much-delayed court appearance.

'Don't worry,' said the assistant inspector, 'Hernandez knows enough English to write her reports. If there is a problem, she always asks one of the local pathologists to assist.

The first post-mortem she conducted was that of a suspected carjacker, Cuthbert 'Baby Face' Vhundura, who had died in police custody the previous month. I had read about his death in the newspaper at the time because his relatives had refused to bury him until the cause of his death had been ascertained. As a result of the stand-off between the relatives and the authorities, Baby Face's body had been in the mortuary for nearly a month until the intervention of a senior Ministry of Health official. One of Baby Face's friends, a burly man with a missing front tooth, asked me whether the police would allow them to witness the post-mortem.

'What do you mean?'

'We want to be there, you know. We want to observe everything.'

'That's very brave of you, but from what I know about these things I don't think the doctor will agree. Why don't you just wait for the results of the post-mortem?'

'It's tricky,' said the burly man in a hushed voice. 'We have some unresolved questions.'

'About your friend's death?'

'Yes.'

'What exactly do you mean?'

'Our friend died in police custody, and that in itself is very suspicious. He was fine when the police arrested him. They shot the tyres of the car he was driving, forcing him to stop. Then they put him in the back of their pick-up truck, handcuffed him to the side of the vehicle and took him to the police station. We strongly suspect they beat him up in his cell at the police station.'

'Causing his death?'

'Nobody knows. That is why we want to be present when the post-mortem is performed. We don't want a cover-up.'

During the course of the morning I learnt that the burly man's name was Clyde. His associate, a small hairy fellow with an impish grin, was called Dhiva, a colloquial corruption of David. Throughout the proceedings Dhiva had a distant expression on his face and said very little. Once, he looked at me, shook his head, and uttered the single word: 'Assault.' Then he lit a cigarette and turned his head away. As the morning wore on Clyde gave me more details of how their deceased friend had met his untimely end.

The previous week Baby Face had been stopped at a roadblock just before the evening rush hour. When the policeman pointed out to him that the car he was driving had fake number plates Baby Face sped off in a huff, knocking down a second policeman who had tried to stop him. Because the vehicle he was driving matched that of one that had been carjacked a few days previously, the police at the roadblock reported the incident to the Vehicle Theft Squad. They also gave detailed descriptions of both the car and its driver.

Later that evening four plainclothes detectives went looking for Baby Face at a nightclub in a high-density township where he was drinking beer with several friends, including Clyde and Dhiva. Baby Face managed to elude the lawmen by jumping through a window and getting into his car. After a high-speed chase through the township's convoluted and potholed streets one of the policemen managed to bring the pursuit to an end when he fired several shots at the speeding car's rear tyres. The vehicle ended up in a roadside ditch but Baby Face clambered out unhurt.

'They arrested him and took him to the police station,' said Clyde. 'The next thing we knew was that he had been brought to this hospital. A few hours later he died. Just like that. Baby Face was fit and went to the gym every day. He was not the sort of person who would just drop dead. Last year another one of our friends died in exactly the same way. It's all very fishy. That's why we want to witness the post-mortem. Somebody has a lot of explaining to do. But tell me about your cousin. What happened to him?'

'He was found dead in a patch of waste ground five kilometres from his house wearing just his socks and underwear. There were bruises on his stomach and shoulders. The police suspect foul play.'

'Could it have been a politically motivated crime? There has been a lot of violence since the March twenty-nine election.'

'Very unlikely; Eldridge had very little interest in politics. His whole life was centred on his wife and two daughters.'

'So, what do you think happened?'

'I don't know. But just like you, I am hoping the post-mortem will give us the answers we seek.'

On our way back to the house that evening I sat in the passenger seat and idly scanned the contents of the post-mortem report, a sparsely worded document of about half a dozen pages written in a barely legible scrawl. There were numbered sub-headings inside the left margin of each page against which the doctor had filled in her comments and findings.

'*I, Dr. Juanita Hernandez, do hereby make and swear that I am a duly Registered Medical Practitioner employed by the Ministry of Health in Zimbabwe as a forensic pathologist...*'

It was only later that night that I would finally get to know what Eldridge had done on that fateful Friday. As we sat around the fire in the back garden of the house one of Eldridge's friends told us what had happened. He said about half a dozen of them had gone to a meeting at a hotel in the city centre to discuss the nationwide violence that had followed the just ended 'harmonised' election. The main opposition party had secretly convened the meeting and it was to be addressed by a newly elected MP. But barely half an hour later riot police had come into the hotel and dispersed the gathering, which they said was illegal. One of the policemen had read out the relevant section of the Public Order and Security Act.

'I should tell you that under POSA the police have the power to disperse disorderly gatherings. They can even use firearms if it becomes necessary...'

Scuffles had broken out and the man said that was the last time he had seen Eldridge. Some of the people who had been at the meeting had later turned up in the cells at Harare Central police station, others had been located at the casualty departments of several hospitals, nursing broken limbs, black eyes and bloodied noses. But of Eldridge there had been no sign. Yet his involvement in politics came as a shock to me. Eldridge had always exhibited a cynical antipathy towards mainstream politics. He wouldn't even be bothered to go and vote during elections, saying it changed nothing and only served as a tool to legitimise what he called the 'status quo'. He justified his cynicism by saying that he couldn't decide whether most African leaders were heroes or looters, nationalists or thugs.

'How many African leaders have left office of their own accord?' He once challenged me.

I could only think of Kenneth Kaunda of Zambia, who had lost an election and, incredulously, humbly accepted the result – and Samora Machel, whose plane crashed mysteriously in the Mozambican bush. Although the jury was still out on what had actually happened to Machel, I could see the point Eldridge was trying to make. I thought I knew him, but perhaps I didn't know him as well as I thought I did. All I was left with was a foggy memory of him on the day he passed that elusive fifth O-Level, sitting on a storm-water drain with a bottle of Castle lager and singing his favourite Bob Marley song: '*We gonna chase those crazy baldheads...*'

After collecting the post-mortem report Simon Pfende and I had gone to the Births and Deaths Registration offices located at the front of the hospital to get the burial order. There was a queue of about half a dozen people and we were only served after about forty minutes. Then we walked all the way to the mortuary at the back of the hospital where the hearse from the funeral home was waiting.

'... *There is approximately two litres of blood in the thoracic cavity, two left side ribs are fractured, left lung is severely lacerated and there are multiple bruises on upper parts of body. Signs of shock in abdominal organs – peritoneum, oesophagus, liver, bladder, kidneys, pancreas and suprarenals...*'

The mortuary attendants brought out Eldridge's body in a metal trolley to the dark airless space in front of the loading bay. One of them lifted the corner of a bloodstained plastic sheet and asked me whether the body was indeed that of my cousin, Eldridge Gunguwo. The man, whom I could tell was a member of the Apostolic Faith from his clean-shaven head and goatee beard, was polite, but in a creepy sort of way. For some reason, he reminded me of a character in a horror movie I'd watched as a youngster. Eldridge's face was serene and peaceful, as if he was sleeping and would soon be up and going about his usual business

'Yes. That is Eldridge Gunguwo.'

The group of men who claimed their colleague had died in police custody were also at the mortuary, collecting his body in an open truck. Two stone-faced elderly women sat in the back of the truck, their lips parched by hunger. The man called Clyde looked at me and said nothing. 'Assault', said his friend Dhiva, before lighting a cigarette and turning his head away.

We drove back to Eldridge's house where his relatives and friends had gathered for the funeral. Melody sat on the floor of the small living room, cuddling her daughter Roxanne and surrounded by female relatives. Auntie Beulah Chikoko, now in the twilight of an illustrious if somewhat controversial life, sat next to Melody's mother with Melody's daughter Maxine on her lap. The previous evening, I had heard auntie Bee consoling Melody by telling her that death was something that came to all of us eventually.

'Be brave, my child. Death is like the rain that falls on the just and the unjust alike.'

On the wall above Melody was a framed photograph of their wedding day taken in Harare Gardens – Eldridge and his new bride standing rigidly next to a white limousine in the bright sunshine of a sub-Saharan autumn. We all knew Melody had been Eldridge's rock, the ever-reliable anchor that stabilised him as he waded through life's turbulent storms. Before he met her he had drifted through a life of unstable short-term relationships.

After I had signed the register at the mortuary the attendant with the goatee beard had given me a worn-out supermarket plastic bag containing Eldridge's personal effects. There wasn't much: a dusty red Liverpool Football Club replica jersey with the name 'Gerard' on the back, a white T-shirt Eldridge liked to wear as an undergarment because of its mildly rude inscription – 'I Can See Uranus', pair of black jeans, Nike running shoes, scraps of paper that had been found in his pockets, a small wallet, a wad of fifty million dollar bearer cheques, a brand new membership card for the opposition party and the twenty-one carat gold chain he had bought during his Johannesburg days. Clearly, this was not a man who had been killed during a botched robbery; the first thing any self-respecting robber would have gone for was that very expensive chain.

I went into the main bedroom and left the plastic bag on the bed.

'*... There is severe bruising on left side of neck and also inside left armpit, lips are swollen, two upper incisors are loose...*'

Eldridge's body was due to arrive later that evening, to lie in view awaiting burial the following afternoon. The female mourners in the house had cleared a space in the small living room for the coffin, next to a framed photograph of a twenty-something Eldridge sporting a spiky hairdo and wearing his favourite T-shirt – the one with the malapropism 'Ruck Fules' emblazoned across the front. His brother Hector, long lost in America, sent Eldridge the T-shirt on his twenty-first birthday. Eldridge loved T-shirts with nonsensical inscriptions. In our teens he had on that said 'Why Can't I Be Rich Instead Of Just Good-Looking?' And to me Eldridge's whole life was like a photographic album, an abstract collage of images freeze-framed in my mind; a story with no discernible linking threads.

I had known Eldridge all my life, yet it had come as a surprise to me to learn that the carefree and happy-go-lucky cousin I had known for all those years and once spent a wild Christmas holiday with in Johannesburg's seedy underbelly had been active in opposition politics. This was a man who took pride in the fact that he had never even voted in his entire life and always insisted all politicians were crooks. According to Eldridge, there were three professions that required a fair measure of ruthlessness, dishonesty and cunning in a man: law, politics and the priesthood. I remember how, after downing a few lukewarm Lion lagers at auntie Bee's, Eldridge joked that if voting changed anything governments the world over would make it illegal. But he reserved his most acerbic comments for the narcissistic rulers of our beleaguered and blighted continent.

'In Africa democracy is not always the will of the people,' he once told me, 'because our leaders like to justify their continued hold on power by telling us that sometimes the majority can be wrong.'

But Eldridge was not always the doom-and-gloom sage of auntie Bee's bottle store and could be quite funny when he wanted to. During our primary school days, we would play five-a-side soccer with a plastic ball at weekends in the dusty street in front of our houses. Sometimes the ball ended up in the backyard of Mr Norbert Ganyire, an irascible civil servant who would only give it back after one of us had gone to the house and apologised profusely. The task of retrieving the ball always fell upon Eldridge, who had gone from being a toddler with an embarrassing speech impediment to a youth who possessed the charm to sweet-talk an Eskimo into buying a fridge.

'What do you say to Mr Ganyire for him to give you the ball back?' I once asked him. He winked and gave a typically cryptic response:

'It all boils down to diplomacy and tact, my friend. Only a fool will use a hammer to bludgeon a flea.'

'... Also observed is a general swelling of facial features, multiple fractures on left side of pelvis, left leg femur and right leg tibia, also fractures on vault and base of skull, blood in nostrils indicative of brain haemorrhaging....'

So now we all knew.

Eldridge had been an active member of the opposition, an unforgivable sin in the turbulent and brutal politics of my country. But what else had he done in his short but adventurous life that none of us knew about? What other secret skeletons lurked in his soon to be permanently closed cupboard? As one of his uncles said as we sat by the fire the previous evening, if a man has one known vice he is likely to have many more unknown ones.

The Eldridge I knew from our Warren Park 'D' days never grew up. Even in adulthood, he still lived a life blithely cocooned in the harmless fantasies of our childhood. He was a man full of jokes, Eldridge, a man full of life and a man with time for everybody. Yet the story of his short and tragic life will always remain a profound conundrum, like one of those giant jigsaw puzzles where the picture only becomes clear when all the pieces are in place.

But when the political stakes are high, life is always cheap.

'... As a result of this forensic examination, I formed the conclusion that the cause of death was blunt force trauma as a direct result of severe assault. The police should investigate...'

8

Sugar

*The broad mass of a people will more easily
fall victim to a big lie than to a small one.*

(Adolf Hitler, *Mein Kampf*)

The rumour had to be true because it had been confirmed by
a woman whose daughter worked as a till operator at the large
supermarket on the edge of the township. At around noon that
day the supermarket would take delivery of a large consignment
of a scarce commodity.

Throughout the morning, as an expectant crowd gathered in
the supermarket forecourt; speculation had been rife as to what the
scarce commodity could be. It couldn't be cooking oil, because for
the previous week the supermarket's shelves had been brimming
with that particular product. Bread, though also sometimes prone
to major shortages, was stacked ceiling high in one corner of the
bakery section. Maize meal had been delivered the previous day
and although most of it had routinely vanished off the shelves in
the mad scramble that followed, a few battered and bruised five-
kilogram pockets still littered the floor next to the dog food section.
By mid-morning, a process of elimination had identified the scarce
commodity to be delivered at noon: sugar. And not just any sugar,
but the sought-after white variety neatly packaged in long-lasting
twenty-kilogram sacks.

Mrs Emilia Mapfumo, a widowed mother of four and
grandmother of eleven who worked as a domestic maid for a white
family in one of the affluent northern suburbs, was on her way to

work that Sunday morning. She heard the rumours of the impending sugar delivery as she waited to board the commuter omnibus that would take her to the city centre. She lived in two rented rooms with four of her grandchildren, including ten-year-old twin boys, Cain and Abel. The boys had been left in her care by her daughter Regina who five years previously had succumbed to that ubiquitous scourge of modern times, the 'slow puncture'.

The twins went to a primary school in the township and each morning their meagre breakfast consisted of maize meal porridge and sometimes, when their grandmother could afford it, tea and a few slices of stale bread. The tea and the porridge needed sugar to make them palatable and Mrs Mapfumo had not had sugar at her house for over two months. She soon became caught in two minds – whether to continue with her journey to work or join the crowd outside the supermarket until the sugar arrived. As she stood at the commuter omnibus ranks in front of the supermarket, grappling with indecision, she was soon joined by Mrs Marjorie Tsvete, a neighbour who ran a thriving flea market in the city centre.

'Sugar is coming at noon,' said Mrs Mapfumo to her neighbour's enquiry.

'Brown?'

'White.'

'That's good news. I haven't had sugar in my house for over two months.'

'Yes, me too.'

'But are you not supposed to be going to work?'

'I'll tell the madam the kombi was stopped for being overloaded. I can't afford to miss this God-given opportunity.'

The two women walked to the font of the supermarket and made themselves comfortable by removing their flip-flops and sitting cross-legged on the *stoep* on the edge of the car park. It was now around ten. People attracted by the rumours of a sugar delivery continued to arrive, milling in high spirits around the car park and enjoying the winter sunshine.

'I wonder how many packets they will allow each person to buy?' said Mrs Tsvete.

'Even just one is good enough for me,' said Mrs Mapfumo. 'Beggars can't really be choosers, you know. If the porridge has no sugar, those twins of Regina's won't touch it.'

'My husband doesn't like sugar,' said Mrs Tsvete. 'He says it gives you diabetes.'

'Men always think about themselves. My late husband Godfrey – may he rest in peace – spent all his money on beer, but in the end what good did it do him?'

Three more women from Mrs Mapfumo's neighbourhood soon joined them. Mrs Edna Garwe, clad in her spotless blue and white United Methodist uniform and on her way to church, decided it was worth her while to wait for the sugar delivery. So did Mrs Nyarai Murindagomo, a vegetable vendor on her way to town to order the tomatoes and onions she sold illegally outside the supermarket. Mrs Sheba Jangano, another vegetable vendor, soon joined them. She too had heard about the impending sugar delivery.

'I thought you had already left for work,' she said when she saw Mrs Emilia Mapfumo.

'I will go after the sugar has arrived.'

'But what will you tell your employer?'

'I will tell the madam one of the twins came down with the chicken pox and I had to take him to hospital.'

'But both the twins had the pox last year…'

'Yes, I know. But the madam doesn't know that.'

'You cannot get the pox twice.'

'The madam doesn't know the twins had the pox last year, so if I told her they have the pox now it doesn't make any difference to her. She doesn't care about my family. That woman is only worried about herself.'

As the crowd around them continued to swell the women stood in the sunshine, exchanging idle gossip. Inevitably, the conversation soon turned to politics. Mrs Sheba Jangano said she had been shocked to read in the newspaper that the ailing ex-president of a country to the north of theirs had been arraigned before the courts for grand theft.

'Forty-six million American dollars is a lot of money. I doubt if any of us can spend even a million dollars in our lifetime.'

'And if you are a president you get everything, so why steal?'

'Some people are just greedy.'

'But you must know that in Africa men become leaders not because they want to better their countries, but because they want to better themselves.'

Mrs Kerestenzia Murindagomo, a staunch supporter of the government, shook her head so vehemently her fluffy mound of grey hair bristled like a windswept cotton field.

'You, Sheba Jangano, are beginning to sound like a member of the opposition.'

'Even if I was, isn't that what democracy is all about?'

At about half past eleven an unmarked truck, its long trailer covered with a plain white tarpaulin, pulled into the delivery yard at the back of the supermarket. Its arrival was greeted with a deafening crescendo of cheers, ululations and catcalls. A small group of women started doing the traditional dance known as *kongonya* in front of the supermarket, sending a whirlpool of choking dust into the air. Fits of uncontrolled coughing erupted as the excited crowd – a heaving, shoving multitude of men, women and children – surged in waves to the front of the supermarket. Some of the supermarket's employees tried to control the unruly throng but they were soon overwhelmed by the sheer size of the crowd. Mrs Mapfumo and Mrs Tsvete, both in their mid-sixties and overweight, quickly found themselves at the back of the huge crowd. In the supermarket's delivery yard, Mrs Mapfumo caught a glimpse of grim-faced men in blue overalls chucking large white bags over the sides of the trailer. Her heart began to pound.

'I'll tell the madam the kombi was involved in an accident. You know how those kombi drivers always drive like demons...'

But Mrs Tsvete did not hear her neighbour amidst all the talking and shouting. From where the two women stood they could see the supermarket's manager talking to the people at the front of the queue. They could not hear what was being said, but they could tell from the young man's gesticulations that whatever he was imparting was not good news.

'I wonder what he's saying,' said Mrs Mapfumo.

'I don't know. Maybe we should move closer.'

As they moved closer to the front of the queue they could see people were already dispersing. A man known to both women walked past, shaking his head and clicking his tongue.

'These people think they can waste our time,' he said to nobody in particular.

'What is the manager saying?'

'The delivery... It's not sugar.'

'No?'

'It's dog food.'

'Dog food?'

'Yes.'

'They make us wait all this time for dog food? Who in the township buys dog food anyway?'

'He said he didn't ask us to come here. He said it's not his fault if people decide to gather outside his shop because of a rumour.'

'But he could have told us a long time ago...'

'He said he told the people at the front of the queue, but nobody believed him. They accused him of trying to disperse the crowd so that he could sell the sugar to his relatives and friends.'

Mrs Mapfumo turned to her neighbour, Mrs Tsvete.

'I better go to work. I'll tell the madam I lost my bus fare to pickpockets and had to walk to work. It's pay-day today. If I don't get the money I have slaved for this past month what will I give those orphaned twins of mine?'

9

A Dirty Game

Politics, as a practice, whatever its professions, has always been the systematic organization of hatreds.

(Henry Adams)

In January 2003, when I was thirteen years old, my eldest sister Bernadette sent us an e-mail saying she was planning to marry a Kenyan doctor she had met whilst studying medicine in England. She said the special wedding invite was on its way and the event itself would take place on Boxing Day in an old stone church in a town called Cambridge, which was near London.

My other sister Primrose and myself had never been to England and were very excited by the news of this proposed event. All I knew about Cambridge was that its university was the source of grief for many teenagers because that was where the O-level exam papers were set. My father, elated by the news that he was finally to have a son-in-law, started making frantic arrangements for the trip even though there was still almost a year to go before the big event.

In 2003 my sister Prim was sixteen years old and in the fourth form at a very expensive Catholic school. Prim was not terribly bright and could never grasp the simplest scientific concepts. Quadratic equations completely baffled her, matrices and geometric transformations made her develop goose bumps and for a long time she couldn't tell the difference between cirrostratus, cirrocumulus and stratocumulus. She also thought mensuration and menstruation were one and the same thing. The only subject she was good at was Fashion and Fabrics, mainly because she spent a fortune on glossy magazines and watched a lot of daytime soap operas.

Even when we watched a film on television Prim was more interested in what the characters were wearing than in the dramatic nuances of the story. She hardly read her books, but preferred to spend her time text messaging her friends on the latest celebrity gossip. She had a pointless but all-consuming interest in the day-to-day adventures of pop and film stars – who was sleeping with who, who had checked into rehab, who had the weirdest sexual fetish and so on and so forth.

Her end of term reports – despite diplomatic phrases like 'tries very hard' and 'needs to unlock her true potential' – pointed to a hopeless student firmly on the path to academic oblivion. But this did not deter her; she harboured vague ambitions of being someone very important in the government when she finished school, just like our father. We all knew she wasn't going to do well in her O-levels and had mentally prepared ourselves for the worst. My mother said even if it meant she had to re-write it wouldn't exactly be the end of the world.

'I know many people whose children have failed exams,' she would say. 'Exams don't mean much these days. Some of the world's most successful people were not very good at school. Everybody knows that America, the world's most powerful nation, has had a failed actor as one of its presidents. Prim has her dreams, and that's good enough for me.'

In a way my mother was right. Everyone who is successful must have dreamed of something.

Bernadette has always been the clever one in our family. In her younger years we used to call her 'Brain Box', a nickname she loathed with a passion. She won prizes from Grade 1 to Grade 7 and sailed through secondary school. She achieved a record breaking five 'A's at A-Level, which was how she had won a scholarship from a British university to study medicine in England. She had even overcome that other notorious pitfall of teenage-hood, the driving test, at her very first attempt.

I remember how at the time she won the scholarship my father greeted the news of her achievement with mixed feelings. On the one hand he was happy for his daughter's good fortune, but on the other, as a senior government official, he resented the fact that her benefactor was a university in Britain. My father didn't like the British, always telling us that they were thieves and plunderers who had stolen the black man's wealth under the guise of religious philanthropy.

'It was the arrival of the Bible that put the black man in chains,' he would moan.

Both Prim and I had gone on holidays with our parents before, but only to regional destinations like Mauritius, Johannesburg, Cape Town and Durban. Because of his important job in the government my father had been to every place on earth that could be reached by passenger plane – Singapore, Guatemala, Malaysia, Egypt, China, Dubai, Bhutan. He once went to Egypt and told us that a blind beggar showed him the exact spot where Moses had parted the Red Sea to escape Pharaoh's wrath. He had even been to Outer Mongolia, a place I only knew as a sprawling mass of hilly outcrops on a relief map of Asia at the school library. But his favourite place was Beijing. He always said the people there were very friendly and the food those Chinese ate was simply amazing. They eat everything, he said, including monkeys, tortoises, sharks, dogs, lizards, cockroaches, cats and snakes. Once, on an official trip to the People's Republic, and much the worse for alcohol, he had been daring enough to try raccoon meat.

'It tastes like chicken,' he told us on his return.

During the second term school holiday we accompanied my father to the British High Commission to make the visa applications. There were many people outside the building and the queue went twice around the block. In 2003 people in my country had to queue for everything because everything was in short supply. Sugar, milk, salt, cooking oil, fuel and, sometimes, even water. Some people we talked to told us they had been in the queue from four o'clock in the morning, waiting to have their papers processed. They had even brought food to eat and novels to read whilst idling away time in the long queue. Our father took one look at the meandering line of bodies, looked at his watch, told us to wait for him and then disappeared inside the building. We were only in the queue for about ten minutes before he came back and asked us to follow him. We immediately knew he had arranged something. My father was a senior government official and he knew many influential people. He always arranged things.

We went into a small office where a balding African gentleman with uneven yellow teeth asked us to fill in some forms while he exchanged idle chat with my father. He asked my father whether he could use his political connections to arrange a large commercial farm for him, preferably one with a dam, or a stream running through it.

'With these recurrent droughts, irrigation is best,' said the bald man.

My father said it was now difficult to get a farm because of the bad publicity in the press about all the people being given farms and not doing anything with them, but he would see what could be done. The bald man, eager to please his would-be benefactor, said the people who were getting land and not utilising it were unwittingly helping the cause of those committed to derailing the government's agrarian reform programme.

'These people are two-faced. They are wolves wearing sheep's clothes,' said the bald man.

'Yes, they are reactionaries working in cahoots with imperialist forces to reverse the gains of our hard-won Independence,' agreed my father.

But my father did not need a visa to go to England. He had a special government passport that allowed him to visit any country in the world any time he wanted to do so. The bald man asked us to sign our visa application forms. I did not yet have a proper signature so I just made up one on the spot – a scrawny and indeterminate mark that Prim took one look at and shook her head in disbelief. When we left, the queue outside the building was twice its original length. Most of the people in it looked weary and dejected, like a demoralised army on the verge of a catastrophic defeat. I was happy I had a father who knew people and could arrange things.

That evening when we got home our mother showed us some pictures of Benny and her Kenyan boyfriend that had come by e-mail. The pictures had been taken when Benny and the Kenyan man had gone on a walking holiday near some Welsh town with an unpronounceable name. I asked Prim why anybody in England would want to go and walk on their holiday when there were all those cars available but she was in a foul mood and just shook her head and clicked her tongue.

'Go and do your homework,' she said.

The Kenyan doctor was a handsome fellow, quite unlike his thin and dark countrymen I had seen chasing steeples or running the marathon at the Olympics in Australia. He had an expansive grin on his face, like a man who had just won the Lotto jackpot. But I felt both relieved and jealous that he was everything I had not imagined him to be.

The months slowly went by and in late October my own excitement, which by then far surpassed everybody else's, reached fever pitch. I badly wanted to go to London to see Piccadilly Circus and Big Ben and all the other things I had seen on television. I dreamt of sunset cruises on the Thames and of having my photograph taken standing next to the famous wax figures at Madame Tussauds. I dreamt of Buckingham Palace and the Tower of London, where our history teacher Mr Gandu told us many members of the nobility had been beheaded for treason and adultery.

'The English used to be ordinary savages,' he explained. 'The French were worse. Did you know they are the ones who invented the guillotine?'

I already knew that, but I didn't want to say so because Mr

Gandu would have accused me of showing off. Mr Gandu did not take kindly to his students knowing things he thought they didn't know. The privilege to impart new historical knowledge was his and his alone. But then as the days dragged by I started to worry about unthinkable possibilities, about things that could go wrong when we least expected them to – what our English teacher Mr Brennan called 'Sod's Law'. It was quite possible my father could have an unwelcome attack of his perennial gout problem a day before our scheduled departure. During these attacks the big toe on his right foot would become tender and pink, like an overcooked beetroot, grounding him for several days and forcing him to go on an herbivorous diet. Sometimes the pain would become so bad he could barely walk.

'It's like walking barefoot on a field of broken glass,' was how he often described the excruciating pain.

Mother would give him an unsympathetic look, put her hands on her hips and just shake her head. At supper she would tell me to eat my greens.

'Men and meat and beer... Now you can see where it all ends.'

But we all knew she didn't really mean what she said. It was just her way of telling him to watch his eating habits. But he never listened. As soon as he was back on his feet it was back to Zambezi lager, T-bones, fried liver and braised oxtail.

There were other subtle variants of Sod's Law that could yet scupper the big event. What if on the day of our departure the plane was inexplicably cancelled or delayed and we had to postpone our trip? What if there was a nationwide fuel shortage and we couldn't even go to the airport? What if mother suffered one of her momentary amnesia bouts and forgot all our passports and tickets at home? What if the Kenyan doctor developed cold feet and decided that our Benny, incredibly beautiful and intelligent as she was, was not the one for him? What if some Kenyan woman he was secretly married to back home in Nairobi turned up on the day of the wedding and actually stood up during the part when the priest challenges those with objections to the marriage to stand up or forever hold their peace, and didn't hold hers? It had happened before, at the wedding of one of my father's cousins. The man's 'small house' turned up unannounced at the reception and caused untold pandemonium. All these things were quite possible, in my view. We did not know the history of the man Benny wanted to marry and all we could do was place our faith in her judgment and hope for the best. After all, as our father always reminded us, Benny was a sensible girl.

One day at school I told my best friend Robert Nhamo that my sister Benny was having a wedding in a big stone church in England and that all of us were flying there at the beginning of the summer holiday for the occasion. I asked him whether there was anything special he wanted me to bring back and he said his brother Kennedy who lived in England had told him everything there was so expensive; maybe the only thing I could afford to bring back for him were chocolates and wine gums from the airport duty-free shops. I said if that were the case I would be happy to just go and see Piccadilly Circus and Big Ben and maybe take pictures on my father's new digital camera to show him. He said I shouldn't get excited for nothing because Piccadilly Circus was not a real circus – there were no lions or trapeze artists or dodgem cars – and Big Ben was just a big clock on a tower at the Houses of Parliament. I could see he was jealous, but he was my friend and I didn't mind him feeling the way he did. I could understand his envy.

A week before the wedding my father came home from work early one evening and dropped a bombshell. He said he'd gone to the British High Commission to check on our visas and been told by his bald friend with the yellow teeth that there had been a slight problem with our applications. He said none of us would be going to the wedding in England. He said even his special government passport that allowed him to visit any country in the world at any time he wanted was no good.

My mother furrowed her brow in disbelief. 'Surely the British can't do that?'

'It's their country and they can do anything they want.'

'But why?'

My father said an organisation called the European Union had put our country on an international list of bad guys and all the people connected in some way to the government were banned from travelling to Europe.

'But we want to go to Britain, not Europe,' mother interjected in the shrill but determined voice she used when having pointless arguments with my father.

'Britain is in Europe, mummy.'

He always called her mummy when he wanted to be really sarcastic. The ban, father added, included spouses and dependants. My mother, though clearly just as disappointed as all of us, thought she had a simple solution.

'Why don't they have the wedding in America? It would be nice to go to New York or Miami.'

My mother had been to a conference in Miami at the invitation of some non-governmental organisation and she often told us of that city's buildings that were painted in every colour of the rainbow. On her way back from that trip she forgot her camera with all the pictures she had taken in the closet of her hotel room.

'We cannot even go to America,' said father. 'There is another list of banned people there and we are also on it.'

'All of us?'

Father nodded his head.

My mother, undeterred, pressed on.

'If we can't go there, why don't they come here? There are many places here where they can have a decent wedding reception. There is the Sheraton, the Holiday Inn, the Botanical Gardens, and even the large hall at my church can be hired for a small fee.'

My father shook his head.

'Benny cannot come here.'

'Why not? This is the country of her birth. Surely, the European Union or whatever it's called can't stop her coming here?'

'I know. But if she comes here she won't be able to go back to England. Her papers there are not in order.'

'In England?'

'Yes.'

'But she has a valid passport...'

'You need other papers to stay in England – a visa and work permit. It's fine if you don't have those things if you're already there. But once you leave the country you can't go back.'

'But she went there on a Rhodes scholarship...'

'It doesn't matter. She finished university two years ago. She is now working, and she does not have a work permit.'

'So?'

'That makes her an illegal immigrant. If they catch her, they will deport her.'

My mother clicked her tongue in disgust. She looked perplexed, like a contestant on a quiz show who keeps getting the answers wrong. But she knew all there was to know about deportations, two of her maternal cousins having been expelled from America for being 'illegal aliens'. One of them, aunt Gertrude, had spent twelve years working as a housemaid for a man whose job was to find and prosecute illegal immigrants.

Mother walked slowly to the kitchen where she was preparing a tuna and avocado salad for herself. She always ate tuna and avocado salads during the hot weather because she claimed it was good for her skin. My mother constantly worried about her skin losing its lustre and her body losing its shape. So she always watched what she ate, and told us what to eat. But the news about the visas had clearly unsettled her. She kept blowing her cheeks and shaking her head. She kept complaining about the many things she did not understand that happened in the world. Why was our country on a list of bad guys and yet we had never done any harm to anybody?

My father pointed out that her observation was not quite true. He told her that we had taken the land back from the white people in the country and their kinsmen in the European Union were punishing us for it. It's not their land, my mother protested. The white people found us here.

'That may be so,' said my father, 'but politics is a dirty game.'

Later that evening I asked Prim whether she thought we could get visas for Benny's wedding if the government gave back some of the land it had taken. I explained to her how it could be done. A formula could be worked out whereby, say, each farm returned to a white farmer would result in one visa being given to a prospective traveller. So, in the case of the four of us who wanted to go to Benny's wedding, the government would give back four farms to the white people. That way, everybody would be happy. It would be what our English teacher Mr Brennan called a win-win situation.

'Don't be silly. The government is not going to give back the land so you and I can get visas to go to Benny's wedding in England. The government people in England don't even know who Benny is.'

'But our father is a senior government official. Everybody knows him.'

'So?'

Prim always supported the government, through thick and thin – through flood or hail. Maybe it was because she harboured vague ambitions to work for the government when she left school.

'You honestly think anybody else apart from us cares about Benny's wedding?'

'Benny is my sister. I care for her, just like I care for you.'

She clicked her tongue and just glared at me.

'You know something?'

'What?'

'You are a very stupid boy.'

We never went to England.

We stayed at home and waited for news of the wedding. Whenever my mother said how unfair the whole visa thing was my father would just shake his head and tell her that politics was a dirty game. Even now he still maintains our failure to go to England was part of a comprehensive package of reprisals by individuals inside the country working in cahoots with vengeful western governments to reverse the gains of our hard-won independence. I discussed the visa issue with my sister Prim on several occasions but, as usual, she would be in one of her foul moods and I could never get anything sensible out of her.

'We have never stopped the white people from coming here, even though they once made us slaves,' I reasoned.

'So what? That was a long time ago.'

'But it's our sister's wedding, Prim. Benny will not be happy if we are not there.'

'Just go and do your homework.'

I secretly hoped there would be a last-minute hitch and then the event would be indefinitely postponed until our government and the European Union sorted out their problems and we got our visas. But the wedding went like clockwork. Benny sent us the wedding video and over a hundred photographs by e-mail; although they were quite interesting it was not the same feeling as actually being there in the flesh, toasting the newly-weds and eating a piece of the wedding cake. And Benny looked so incredibly beautiful in her lily-white wedding gown my mother wanted to cry.

'Just look at her,' she sighed, 'floating like an angel.'

Last month Benny sent my mother an e-mail saying she is expecting any time soon. She said she went for a scan and they told her it was a boy. They are going to call him Uhuru, which in Swahili means freedom. Prim said she does not understand why people find out the sex of unborn babies. She says it takes out all the fun out of childbirth. It's like knowing in advance the grades you will get for the O-Levels, she argued. As I have already said, Prim is not terribly bright. And we don't need her brain scanned to know what grades she will get for her O-Levels.

Because my country is still on the European Union's list of bad guys we cannot go to England to see Benny and the baby, when it eventually comes. As for me, it's bye-bye Piccadilly Circus, bye-bye Big Ben, bye-bye London Zoo, bye-bye Ten Downing Street. And because Benny's papers are still not in order there in England she cannot come here and see us. We will just have to make do with a video and pictures of baby Freedom, just as we had to make do with the video and pictures of the wedding in the big stone church in Cambridge. Perhaps our government and the British will work out their problems. Now, that would be a real win-win situation. But somehow, I don't think it will happen any time soon.

Like my father always says, politics is a dirty game.

10

Butternut Soup

I do not know whether there are gods, but there ought to be.

(Diogenes the Cynic)

On the 14th of October 2005, at about half past six in the evening, my wife Hilda hurled a soapstone ashtray at the television in the lounge because I would not let her watch 'The Jerry Springer Show', one of her favourite programmes.

The screen shattered into a thousand little pieces, promptly shutting up motor-mouth Jerry and for the rest of the evening plunging the house into an eerie silence. Hilda stormed out of the room and locked herself up in the bedroom to begin one of her marathon sulks. There was no more television. No more Generations, no more Oprah, no more Movie Magic, no more Big Brother Nigeria.

There has always been a simple solution to the television wars in our house: buying a second set and putting it in the main bedroom. But there is hyperinflation and everything costs so much these days. And a second television is not really a necessity in a household with two people. It's also a good thing there are no children, otherwise our problems would have been greatly compounded. We have been married twelve years but we never had children. The only

114

children who sometimes visit us are Hilda's sisters' daughters and my younger brother's sons.

I have a teenage son from my first marriage, Bruce, but he doesn't get on with Hilda and hardly comes to the house. He lives with his mother and I haven't seen him for almost three years now. After two successive miscarriages early in our marriage Hilda sunk into a lengthy depression. She blamed herself for her womb's periodic malfunctions. She said perhaps there was something wrong with her body, that the miscarriages were punishment for some terrible sin she had unknowingly committed early in her life. Maybe that was why she turned to religion – the Hand Of Faith Pentecostal Church and Pastor Johannes Dollar.

We quarrel a lot in the house, mainly about who watches what on television. Sometimes we come close to exchanging blows, to punching the living daylights out of each other. But she always wins. I always give in. Where there is a master, there will always be a slave.

October 14th 1994.

We got married in court. She said she didn't want a big ceremony. It wasn't. There were two of her relatives and one of mine, an elderly rheumatic aunt long widowed. The officiating magistrate had flu; we could hardly hear what he was saying. *'In sickness and in health, for richer or for poorer. Till television do us part…'*

That should have been our wedding vow.

Television is a wonderful invention. The television remote is an omnipotent device. Having it in one's possession opens up a world of limitless possibilities. In war, it is equivalent to securing a strategic bridgehead or having a machine-gun nest right above the enemy's major supply line. In our house it is like having the power of creation at one's fingertips.

Hilda, who is a civil servant, usually comes home earlier than me and after putting a lump of chicken or pork to defrost in the microwave she sits directly in front of the television, remote control in one hand, plate of boiled peanuts on her lap, Nokia 6110 cellular phone on charger nearby. Her entire existence seems to revolve around twenty-first-century technology. Having grown up amidst abject hardship, she seems determined to make up for a toy-less and doll-less upbringing. But much as she does not want to be disturbed when watching television, she still cannot fully let go of the world outside her window. The volume is always deafening.

'*And de name of de ninth House Mate to be evicted from de Big Brother Nigeria House is...*'

It is four days after the ashtray incident. No Jerry, No Oprah, no Judge Judy. Hilda is irritable and abrasive, like somebody with a pain the source of which cannot be pinpointed. She is in the throes of chronic withdrawal symptoms. I know the signs. I keep out of her way. Like a fish bruised by a passing crocodile's teeth, I keep to the relative safety of the shallows.

'...... *Joseph!' You have one minute to get out of de Big Brother House, Joseph...*'

She wants to break the ice, she wants our lives to move forward, but she knows I am the wronged party and it is her pride that will have to be sacrificed. There is no such thing as a bloodless truce in our household. Every passing blow leaves an indelible bruise. But my wife is proud and does not easily make concessions, neither does she willingly submit to humility. Both of us know sooner or later, the deadlock of this silent war will have to be broken. But power cannot be shared; there can only be one master in the house.

'... *You have exactly thirty seconds to get out of the Big Brother Nigeria House, Joseph...*'

I work for an insurance company in the city. For over twenty years I have been selling insurance – motor, household, life. In fact, anything that falls outside that grey area known in my industry as *force majeure*. Most of the times I phone up complete strangers, make appointments to go and see them, and then try to convince them that life insurance is good for them. A lot of them give me a polite but firm cold shoulder:

'But if I'm dead, what good is all that insurance money to me?'
'It will benefit your wife.'

'My wife is late.'

'Your children, perhaps?'

'Those layabouts must learn to stand on their own two feet, like all of us. They will inherit nothing from me.'

It is like trying to sell a comb to a bald man.

The decisive phase of the television war started about a month ago. I call it 'The Final Push'. It was the day of the big game, Liverpool versus Chelsea – two bull elephants squaring up in the sulphurous sunshine of an English winter. But there was another eviction coming up on Big Brother, and Hilda wanted to watch that. Her favourite House Mate was a potential candidate for eviction. Because neither of us would budge, we compromised and watched a beauty pageant, 'Miss Rural Woman', on the local channel.

But I had a miserable afternoon.

I was forced to keep track of the score in the big game by phoning my friends, much to their annoyance. But by giving in so easily I had set an ugly precedent. Every evening when I came back from work I would find Hilda sitting by the television in the lounge. And always, the volume would be turned up to maximum, as if she is hard of hearing or something. Hilda loves Reality TV, especially the tackier sort. The noisier and rowdier it is, the more she likes it. There is Oprah, and then there is Jerry Springer. If Oprah is for intellectuals, then Jerry is definitely for certified imbeciles.

'*Jerry, Jerry, Jerry…*'

Television has its good moments in our house; not many, but quite a few. When Hilda is away at her sister's on Saturday afternoons I can buy half a dozen Castle Pilsner lagers and watch the English Premier League 'live', courtesy of the wonders of digital satellite television – Spurs, Arsenal, Newcastle, Aston Villa and, of course, my favourite team, Liverpool. The Reds. 'You Will Never Walk Alone,' I always sing along with the Kop End. Last week the Kop was in good voice; we thumped the opposition four-nil.

And had it not been for television, Hilda and I would probably not have discovered our life's calling – membership of Pastor Johannes Dollar's Hand Of Faith Pentecostal Church. It happened quite by chance. One day Hilda, as was her wont, was idly flicking across the channels and wham – there he was, Pastor Johannes Dollar, as big and as imposing as a morgue door, clad in a spotless white suit complete with matching gloves and silk handkerchief, the sweat dripping down his face as he told the story of King Solomon and the two harlots who went to the famous biblical king disputing the maternal ownership of a newborn infant.

'A child cannot be shared. If she says it's hers, then so be it. But our Lord is there to be shared. His love is so bounteous all of us can have a piece of it.'

This enigmatic servant of the Lord enthralled both of us. Up to that point in my life I had been an unrepentant atheist, believing there is nothing before birth and there is nothing after death. But the pastor changed all that. Pastor Johannes knew how to talk on television, he knew how to convince people to abandon the path of wickedness and seek the salvation of Eternal Life.

It's a Sunday morning, the first day of winter. The pastor is on television, whipping up the emotions of his compliant flock in his usual fire-and-brimstone style. Today he is talking of Armageddon, the Second Coming – the Apocalypse. Hilda's eyes moisten with admiration.

'He has a lot of energy for somebody over seventy,' she says.

'I didn't know he was over seventy.'

'He is.'

'Yes,' I reluctantly agree, having been corrected, 'he has a lot of energy.'

'We must join that man's church,' says Hilda. And that's all she talks about for the next few days, joining the septuagenarian pastor's church. She can be terribly pedantic – a blinkered, one-track-minded animal. She is just like her mother, who is eighty-seven years old although so well preserved one would think she is on the right side of fifty. Hilda's mother has been widowed for ten years. She lives alone in a remote village in the Eastern Highlands and some weekends we drive over to see her. We take her groceries – bread, chicken, flour, sugar and potatoes. Nowadays these basic commodities are like gold dust. And to an old widow living alone anything edible must be like manna from heaven.

When Hilda's mother starts talking she cannot stop. But it's to be expected of one so advanced in her years. As a tribe in central Africa says: when you are very old, you speak like you did when you were very young. She is always talking about her husband, Erasmus. Hilda's father died ten years ago after a long battle with cancer. Hilda had nursed him for the last seven years of his life but when he passed on she was too shattered to attend the funeral.

'You don't want to remember the way somebody died. You want to remember the way they lived,' she said.

When we get back to our house from visiting her mother I read the newspapers and Hilda sits in front of the television, watching the Nigerians playing cards.

'This Big Brother Nigeria is not very exciting,' she says. 'They all talk at the same time and you can't really understand what they are saying.'

'That's how Nigerians speak, Hilda.'

'I know that's how Nigerians speak. Maybe they should put subtitles or something.'

'Maybe.'

Pastor Johannes Dollar.

He is always in the newspapers or on television, donating to this or that charity, embarking on this or that crusade, meeting this or that politician. And he has such boundless energy; he has run three marathons for charity in the past year alone. And this is a man who is well over seventy and has had a heart by-pass. Hilda says that the pastor's amazing energy shows that he is a truly focussed man.

And she says it is because of his charisma that the church's congregation has increased three-fold in less than two years. There is talk of building a new church to accommodate the new converts. Every Sunday there is a special collection for the Building Fund.

The land is already there and the building plans are there, all that is left is the money to put up the structure. And that is where we, the congregation, come in.

But there might be a slight hitch.

The year 2000 was a good television year for both of us. We both love sports, the Sydney Olympics was on ad infinitum, and so there were few fights over what to watch. Sometime we couldn't agree on whether to watch the synchronised swimming or the gymnastics. There was one Russian girl who was exceptionally good on the parallel bars. But we both agreed she was not as good as Nadia, the young Romanian from the 1976 Montreal Olympics. I also like watching test cricket. I can follow the scoring, but I still have to master the strange terminology – deep square leg, silly mid-on, silly mid-off. After years of assiduously following the game I still can't tell the difference between pace and swing, between a 'yorker' and a full toss.

But when the Olympics finished, it was back to Oprah and Jerry.

'Today we are talking to some transvestites and what they think of their controversial lives...'

'The word transvestite is offensive, Jerry. I prefer to call myself a cross-dresser. And I think God meant for me to wear women's clothes...'

'Why?

'I don't know, but all of us have our predetermined destinies.'

This is the hitch.

Last week Pastor Johannes was in the newspapers for all the wrong reasons. A woman who used to belong to the church said he sexually molested her. We all know it is utter nonsense, just the sour grapes of a spurned and vindictive woman. There were special prayers at the church for the pastor, so that the Lord can save him from the satanic machinations of this woman, and there were also prayers for the woman, so she too can also be delivered from her demons. But while the police investigate, the Pastor has to spend the weekend in the cells. It's demeaning, but as Hilda says, those who love the Lord sometimes show their love by accepting such sacrifices.

'Look at the way our Lord suffered for us on Golgotha.'

It's been a long day. I am tired. I say nothing.

Saturday

Downstairs Hilda is watching television by herself. She always seems mesmerised by the crassness and vulgarity of some of the late afternoon programmes. After an unexplained hiatus, Jerry Springer is back in full living colour and I note grimly that the programme has lost none of its tacky garishness and voyeuristic appeal.

'I was a cross-dresser, yes. Bisexuality is not a behavioural aberration, and that is why I am all for same-sex marriages. It is quite possible for animals of the same species to sometimes have divergent biological urges. I'm attracted to men because I was meant to be attracted to men, I guess.'

'And you're not ashamed of what you do?'

'Why? Are you ashamed of what you do?'

'Let me ask the questions.'

'Oh fuck off, you prick...'

'Jerry, Jerry, Jerry...'

The Pastor is out.

It was on the television news. The police have dropped all charges against Pastor Johannes. They have apologised to him, they have apologised to his church. The police spokesman said they would not prosecute because there is insufficient evidence to lay charges. People from the church had gone to the magistrates' courts in anticipation. The television pictures show two hundred, maybe three, milling on the steps of the court building, ululating and clapping their hands. The pastor, pale and unshaven, gives a small speech thanking everybody who stood by him and then announces his engagement to one of the Hand Of Faith usherettes. There is more ululating and clapping of hands.

'Look at all those people,' says Hilda in admiration. 'It's so beautiful. Maybe we should have gone to court.'

'Yes,' I reluctantly agree. 'Maybe we should have gone to court.'

The following evening, at Hilda's invitation, the pastor and his bride-to-be come to our house for dinner. She is shy and pretty, with a radiant childlike innocence. The pastor comments on Hilda's butternut soup, saying it's one of the tastiest things he has ever eaten.

'Back in Ghana, my mother used to make pepper soup. Only this butternut soup is a thousand times better.'

It is a cold Monday evening.

We have now been without a television for exactly four weeks. For Hilda, civilisation as she knows it has come to an abrupt standstill. She might just as well be dead to the world. She finally asks the question I have been expecting.

'Damascus, when are you going to buy another television?'

'Televisions are expensive these days. There is inflation; everything is expensive.'

'I know, but we cannot live in a house without television.'

'Maybe you should have thought about that before you threw the ashtray.'

There is silence.

She is trying to control her breathing, but I can feel her anger rising. Soon, the lava will burst through the fissures onto the ground. A whole month of no Oprah, no Jerry, no Generations, now it's beginning to tell. She is like a drug addict going cold turkey.

'I am sorry.'

'I didn't quite catch that?'

I had heard what she said, but this is my moment of triumph and I want to savour it to the last. Her voice is trembling with anxiety, but the sound of her discomfort is sweet music to my ears.

'I am sorry, Damascus.'

Talking of lava, I once watched a programme about volcanoes – 'The Crucibles of Creation'. I didn't know that volcanic lava is capable of dissolving a human body. But come to think of it, humans are seventy per cent water. Living near a volcano is like having a house next to an unexploded bomb. Hilda is like a volcano; you never know when she is going to erupt.

It's the end of the month.

I know a downtown shop that sells cheap Chinese goods – zhing-zhongs, people in this country call them. The owner is a fat, talkative Indian who smokes foul-smelling cigars. He is willing to let me take out a twenty-nine-inch flat screen on payment of fifty per cent deposit and the remainder to be payable in three equal monthly instalments. What's worse, I have to make payment in American dollars. It's a cumbersome financial burden but I think Hilda has learnt her lesson. When the zhing-zhong television is delivered to the house she stands by the front door smiling.

It's the first time I have seen her smile in weeks.

Saturday afternoon.

The pastor's wedding at a five-star city centre hotel is live on television. The church has paid for the live broadcast, all three hours of the reception. It's rare for us to sit and watch the same television programme together. But the wedding is one of the society events of the year. A lot of dignitaries are there, politicians, media personalities and many wealthy and influential businessmen. Hilda points out the local celebrities as they troop into church. There's so-and-so, there is such-and-such. The bride finally arrives, as pretty as a flower.

'Pastor Johannes has chosen well,' Hilda says, fighting back a sentimental tear.

'She's quite pretty,' I agree.

After the church service the wedding party arrives at the hotel in a fleet of white limousines. Red and pink balloons fly from strings attached to the sides of the vehicles. Two cars are carrying the bridesmaids and the groomsmen. One is carrying his relatives and another is carrying her relatives. Her name is Candid Francisca. She is eighteen years old and comes from Pastor Johannes's home town in Ghana. Her parents sent her to the country after she finished school to be one of the usherettes in the church. There has been a special fund collected for the happy couple's honeymoon on a serene and picturesque Indonesian island.

'Maybe we should have gone to the wedding,' says Hilda.

'Maybe.'

Tuesday.

It is three days after the pastor's wedding. There is a terrible story in the newspapers. A former member of the Hand Of Faith Congregational Choir is claiming the pastor sexually molested her in his office. The woman is married and has five grown-up children. The story comes out on the lunchtime television news – in full, unadulterated zhing-zhong colour.

'He fondled my breasts,' she tells the interviewer.

'Pastor Johannes?'

'Yes. Him.'

'She is at least sixty,' says Hilda, clicking her tongue in disgust. 'Somebody must have put her up to it.'

The twenty-nine-inch zhing-zhong works brilliantly.

We have agreed on a tentative arrangement as to who watches what and when. It is an acceptable arrangement, for now. Hilda has opted for the early evening programmes and the Sunday night movies. I have gone for Saturday afternoons and weekday nights to accommodate my preferred dose of football and crime. 'Forensic Detectives', 'The FBI Files' and 'Cold Case Files'. I also watch the Discovery channel because I enjoy the way it chronicles mankind's follies throughout the ages.

The National Geographic channel is interesting and the History channel is a bottomless repository of fascinating trivia. I have learnt that there is a type of lizard that squirts blood from its eyes to deter predators, and that in some ancient Asian cultures stupidity was actually considered a sophisticated form of intelligence. For scores of years, morons and imbeciles were venerated as deities. I have also learnt how nature compensates for the apparently arbitrary manner with which it apportions natural disasters.

What might seem an advantage one day might be a disadvantage the next. For example, if you build your house on a hill you might be safe from floods. But if there is an earthquake you have a long way to go to the bottom. There is another 'Big Brother' series coming up soon. That's all Hilda. The FIFA World Cup is coming up in June. That's all me. We have to wait and see what happens then.

But there are no more soapstone ashtrays in the living room.

The next day another woman comes forward.

'I'm a cleaner at the church,' she says. 'One day the pastor called me to his office and then unzipped his trousers. I ran away.'

'Why?'

'I knew what he had in mind. I wasn't born yesterday, you know.'

'Why didn't you report this to the police?'

'I was afraid of losing my job.'

'And you are not afraid of losing your job now?'

'No. When that married woman came forward, I also felt strong enough to come forward. These things must come out. The pastor has to respect the fact that we are decent women, that we also have husbands and families.'

'And what about those people saying you are only doing this to tarnish the pastor's name?'

'What would I gain by tarnishing his name? I'll probably lose my job after this, but at least I will sleep soundly in my bed.'

'And what would you say to other women who have been molested but haven't yet come forward?'

'They must come forward. They must tell the truth and shame the devil. That is what the pastor himself says in church. These bad things must come out.'

The television news breaks for a commercial.

'Why do these people tell such lies?' says Hilda shaking her head.

'There is no smoke without fire,' says her sister Perseverance, who has visited for the day together with her two small children.

'Come on, Percy. The pastor would never do something like that.'

'Why not? He is a man, isn't he?'

'Meaning all men are the same?'

'Meaning all creatures of the same species share the same biological impulses. Let's wait for justice to take its natural course.'

Perseverance is very clever. She has a university degree from England but sometimes she does not see eye to eye with her sister. So I am not the only one who disagrees with Hilda.

The newsreader introduces a police spokesman who reads from a prepared statement:

'Yes, it is true that we are currently looking into allegations of sexual molestation against Pastor Johannes Dollar of the Hand Of Faith church. Several women have come forward and given statements to the police regarding this matter. Our investigations are still proceeding but it will be only after we have completed them that we will decide what happens next. That is all I can say at the moment.'

'How many women have actually come forward at this point in time?'

'As of this morning nine women had made statements to the police.'

'And are all these women from the Hand Of Faith church?'

'I am not at liberty to disclose that information as it might prejudice our investigations.'

'What are the charges the pastor is likely to face when your investigations are complete?'

'I am not at liberty to disclose that information as it might prejudice our investigations.'

'Are these complainants single or married women?'

'I am not at liberty to disclose that....'

'Thank you, sir, I think now maybe we should move on to our next news item...'

All work on the new church has stopped. It had reached roof level. Local vandals, like vultures attracted to a fresh carcass, have already attempted to rip out some of the window frames. Ever since the pastor made the headlines, Sunday morning service collections have dropped to a pittance. The contractor has moved off site because of non-payment. And that is not all; he has threatened to take the church to court. The pastor has been in remand prison for five weeks. His lawyers cannot get him bail because on every occasion the state prosecutor objects.

'The accused is a powerful and influential person. It is quite possible he can intimidate or interfere with witnesses. He is also a foreigner and might abscond if granted bail. We request he be denied his freedom in this particular instance, your Worship.'

Some members of the church have been to see the pastor in prison. They say despite the known hardships of the remand prison he is coping remarkably well and prays constantly for deliverance.

'I wanted to cry when I saw him,' said one devotee after going to the prison. 'Can you imagine – they made him wear khaki prison garb just like the other prisoners…'

'To the people who have put him there he is just another prisoner.'

'Yes, there is nothing special about a person once he is in prison.'

When the trial gets underway the prosecution produces its key witness, a twenty-one-year-old woman who now lives abroad. She says she came all the way from California to testify against the pastor. She refuses the court's offer of anonymity.

'He took everything from me. I have nothing to hide anymore.'

In court she drops the bombshell.

'He was friends with my parents. I have known him since I was seven. His daughter used to be my best friend. He used to come to our house a lot when I was young. Six years ago the pastor raped me at his house when my parents left me with him one afternoon. I had to have a back-street abortion two months later.'

'Did you report the rape?'

'No.

'Why not?'

'I was fifteen. Nobody would have believed me.'

There is pandemonium in the public gallery. The magistrate loses control and adjourns court. Later that evening, I notice Hilda's eyes are moist and reddened. Clearly, she has been crying. I have never cried as an adult. Hilda once said that my tears are so distant they must be in my feet,

'Maybe in a moment of weakness the pastor made an error of judgment,' says Hilda, clutching at straws. 'He is only human, after all.'

I wanted to assure her that worse errors of judgment have been made, like *Time* magazine naming Hitler its 'Man of the Year' in December 1938, nine months before he became the twentieth century's most notorious killer.

'That's true. The pastor is only human.'

'The people at church are angry,' she continues. 'If they don't handle this whole thing carefully it can blow up in their faces and a lot of people will be embarrassed.'

Yes. And there will be blood on the floor.

Day six.

Statutory rape carries a mandatory custodial sentence. Things don't look good for the pastor. The prosecutor is a young man straight out of law school. Ruthless and methodical, he is keen to impress, to win promotion to the next rung of his ambitions. Some members of the church keep vigil outside the court, wailing like sinners on Judgment Day. Hilda and I stay at home and keep our fingers crossed. We follow the proceedings on the television news. We both agree the pastor is a good man. He cannot go to jail; the world will be a worse place without him. But after a two-week trial he is convicted, and gets nine years.

'Society has to be protected against monsters like you,' says the magistrate in his summing up.

Nine years.

There is gloom and disbelief outside the court. Candid Francisca, the pastor's teenage bride, is whisked away sobbing hysterically in the back seat of a black Mercedes. Bride and groom were due to leave for the serene and picturesque Indonesian island the following day. But all that is now water under the bridge.

'Of course, he will appeal,' says Hilda's sister Perseverance.

'Yes, he will,' sighs Hilda, emotionally drained.

'We should have been at the court,' I offer lamely.

'Yes,' says Hilda, 'maybe we should have been at the court.'

Printed in the United States
By Bookmasters